SMALL TOWN

PUNK

SMALL TOWN
PUNK

a novel

John Sheppard

BROOKLYN, NEW YORK

Printed in Colombia
Second Paperback Edition
10 9 8 7 6 5 4 3 2 1

Please direct inquires to:
Ig Publishing
178 Clinton Avenue
Brooklyn, NY 11205
www.igpub.com

Sheppard, John L. (John Lawrence)
  Small town punk : a novel / John L. Sheppard.
    p. cm.
  ISBN-13: 978-0-9771972-5-5
  ISBN-10: 0-9771972-5-5
  1. Nineteen eighties--Fiction. 2. Teenagers--Fiction. 3.
Brothers and sisters--Fiction.
  4. Sarasota (Fla.)--Fiction. I. Title.
  PS3619.H458S63 2006
  813'.6--dc22
                                        2006033940

For Nancy

Thanks to artist Vincenzo Murphy, for all the mixtapes, and writer-editor Mike Newirth, for his relentless support.

Contents

One-two-three-four,
ONE-TWO-THREE-FOUR!

Wasted

We'd all gotten beer drunk, and things had gotten out of hand, and now the car was stuck in a drainage ditch on the side of the road. It was Albino's car, so nobody but him seemed to care. Dave said, "beer's warm." He sipped and winced to demonstrate. It was hot and muggy even though it was night. It was always hot and muggy, it seemed. We were gagging on life, trying to wash it away with cheap beer.

"Why don't you go fuck yourself?" Albino asked, leaning on the left front fender.

"No need to go all hostile," Sissy said. Her hair hung oily damp around her face, dirty blond.

"What the fuck happened?" Albino asked, throwing his hands up, sloshing his beer. He took the last swig and tossed the can over his shoulder. It bounced once off the Cougar's hood and toppled into the mud.

"What a bunch of he-men," Sissy said. Her arms were wrapped around her body. She didn't like her small breasts.

"What do we do now?" I asked. I was a little drunker than the rest of them.

"Don't be stupid," Sissy said.

"Show some leg," Dave said. "Maybe we can hitch a ride." He had a silly mustache. He was too skinny. We all were.

"Seen a car lately, dumbass?" Sissy asked him. There weren't even streetlights out here. We were on the Bee Ridge Extension, out in the eastern part of the county. Off to the west we could see the dull glow from Sarasota. Beyond Sarasota was the Gulf of Mexico. We could almost hear the freshly built Interstate. A Cessna droned over Myakka Swamp to the east, probably dropping off a bale or two.

Albino had just bought the car for a thousand bucks. His parents had fronted him half the price and he took care of the rest. He liked the blinkers, which did this dot dot-dot thing. And the Cougar had a 351 Cleveland under the hood. The brakes were shot, though. To stop, he had to grind gears or pull the emergency brake. A little beer, a little let's-see-how-fast-she'll-go, and there we were in a drainage ditch.

"Is anyone holding?" Dave asked.

"We have to get out of this ditch," Albino said. He seemed more pale than usual under the glowing three-quarter moon. His eyelashes flickered. "You guys get behind and push."

"They're only three beers left," I said, peering into the front seat. Someone had ordered an anchovy pizza and my fingers were fishy. We were all wearing red smocks and black pants, plastic nametags with stuck-on tape machine nametapes, and yeasty, garlicky stink. We all worked at the Bee-Ridge Pizza Hut.

The AC/DC coming out of the battered car radio sounded badly out of tune. *"Dirty deeds and they're done dirt-cheap..."*

"Stems and seeds," Sissy commented bitterly. "That's all you guys ever have."

There were no houses out this way, just scrub palmetto, Australian pines and the Sarasota County Landfill, a blue flame and stench cloud of rot near the bend in the road a half mile back. That was where the Bee Ridge Extension began and Bee Ridge Road ended. The Bee Ridge Extension was deserted and straight, perfect for drag racing.

Dave licked his index fingertips and slicked up his peach fuzz mustache.

"Why does this happen to me all the time?" Albino whined.

I leaned through the open window of the two-door and tried to reach for the beer. My feet left the ground, but I still couldn't reach it. The cans had rolled toward the opposite side of the car. Gravity. Sissy bench-pressed my knees up and then I slid most of the rest of the way in.

"Grab me one, too," she said.

"You wearing a bra?" Dave asked my sister.

"I'm not jerk-off material," Sissy said.

Now Albino was interested in something other than his car. "You're not wearing a bra?"

"I'm flat," Sissy said. "Anybody have a smoke? A toke?"

"A joke, a Coke," I said, giggling and reaching around blindly underneath the seat. There had to be more beer. We couldn't have guzzled it all.

"C'mon, Buzz," Dave said to me through the open window. His face was next to my feet, half-obscured by sparkless work shoes that were gummed up with grease and bits of pizza. The one eye that showed was tippled by greedy lust. "I let you see my sister's tits."

I could see underneath the dash, and there were wires and wires all meshed and spooled around. Crazy. Then I felt something cold. A loose beer! Physics, or something, must have kept it cold. I fingertipped it closer until I was able to grab it. A warm can of beer was under my neck, but I didn't care anymore. "Victory," I said as I yanked my feet inside and sat up on the passenger's side floor mat, crushing and exploding the beer can underneath me. Warm beer foamed around my ass.

"Way to go, Buzz," Sissy said flatly.

I popped the top on the cold one and drank lustily. They were all peering in at me now—through the windshield, through the little back window, through the rolled down window—wondering at my drunk. It was a good drunk. It would be a shame to spoil it.

"There're still two left," I said. "Somewhere around here." It was true about Dave's sister's tits. I was over at their house, a three-bedroom shitbox, fucking around with their cable box, the type with the pushbuttons on top. I'd once seen this guy descramble HBO by jamming toothpicks into the buttons, which made them stay half up/down, and made the zigzags on the screen go away. Dave sat on the couch watching me, telling me it was no use. HBO was all T&A in those days—Morey Amsterdam burlesque shows with strippers taking bubble baths in huge champagne glasses. Dort sashayed into the room wearing a red tube top and cutoffs. She had sad hair and marble eyes, boney shoulders and a bruisey mouth.

"Hey, Buzz," she said.

I glanced over at her, a toothpick stuck between my incisors, as Dave leapt to his feet and whipped down her top. She shrieked. (It was more like a yip.) Her banana tits quivered and bounced. For a slim moment she hesitated, like she wanted me to have a nice look. Then her arms swept up to cover herself and she ran from the room, her flip-flops slapping against her soles. I stood there for a flash, a heroin jolt dancing through me. Dave slumped down to the couch, horseshit smile, and tried to light the rest of a roach his mother had left in a souvenir ashtray on the burn-scarred coffee table. His BicClic sparked but wouldn't flame. "You perv," I said at last.

He shrugged and gave up, tossing the lighter behind the couch. "You got a light?" he asked, still smiling like a maniac. "A match maybe?"

"I gotta piss," I said, and reached up to pull on the door handle. The heavy door swung open quickly, and I went for a tumble onto the grass and mud. I pulled myself up using the door and stumbled out into the palmetto bushes to take a hot piss, chugging and spilling my beer as I swayed along.

"Watch out for the snakes!" Sissy shouted after me.

"*You* better watch out for the snakes!" I shouted back. I was clever. I laughed. I stopped at a small clearing and commenced my leak, dropping the empty onto a gray clump of Spanish moss that had fallen out of a tree. "School tomorrow. School, school, school." I closed my eyes as the piss poured out of me. The world swirled around me. "C'mon," I heard Albino plead. It wouldn't work. Sissy had no use for pestering.

We couldn't stay out all night because of school. Not that our parents would notice. They were so at each other's throats that they didn't notice much of anything. I was thinking about moving out and not telling them. I was close enough to eighteen that it wouldn't matter to the authorities. I could make it on the Pizza Hut money.

I walked back to discover the car not in the ditch and

Sissy driving. I ran up to the passenger door and ducked into the back seat behind Albino. "How'd you get it out?" I asked.

"Testosterone," Sissy replied.

"We were challenged, and we rose to it," Dave said, his face all blurred. "Now show us your tits."

"Maybe later," Sissy said. She lit a cigarette, her third of the night. Not that I was counting. She spun the car around expertly on the little two-lane blacktop, and gunned the engine. "Hand me one of those warm beers, or we're going right back into the ditch." A beer was found, and popped open.

"You didn't promise them ..."

"Desperate times, little brother," she said, peering into the rearview at me. "Don't look so upset. It's only these two."

I wasn't her little brother. She only treated me that way.

"Your sister, man," Dave said, shaking his head, smiling like he did the day he undressed his sister for me.

We went back to Pizza Hut. Sissy parked the car near the dumpster out back and we all piled out, tossing empties around, listening to them clink on the pavement. Sarasota pretty much shuts down after 9 p.m. We were inside before we knew what we were doing. We could have asked existential questions. Why are we back at work?

Shit like that. Maybe that's how existentialism started up. It was some sort of fucked up homing signal, like carrier pigeons flying back to their masters in the battlefield.

We took over a booth. Dave went over to the tap and poured us out a pitcher of beer. Janet, the manager, didn't give a shit. She wanted to get fired, maybe take over a kitchen at a rest home. She was a retired army staff sergeant, mess cook.

We sat in the empty restaurant drinking beer out of red plastic cups, not saying much, sharing an ashtray. We thought about playing quarters. The little candle on the table went out, leaving a thin plume of smoke. Dave sat next to Albino, across the table from us. "Gotta take a leak," I said, and Sissy scooted, allowing me out. I stumbled over to the bathroom. Corporate cartoon Pizza Hut Pete, twirling a saucer of dough, glued to the door. Above the urinal my contribution to the bathroom graffiti: GOD IS A BEAR. I wondered what I meant.

In the mirror, razor cuts in the glass left over from our coke-addled ex-assistant-manager. My red-yellow eyes receded in my head. A smile through thin cracked lips.

Out of the bathroom, the floor threatened to smash me in the face. Dave had broken into the Galaga machine with the pliers we used to take the pizzas out of the oven. He'd given himself twenty quarters worth of credit. I could see Janet in the back of the kitchen, smooching her cutesy, grass-dealing girlfriend, whom she'd hired as a waitress. I had such a crush on her, too, the waitress. Cindy. Every time I saw her, I wanted to press myself against her. She gave me this look sometimes like maybe she felt the same way about me. *It's just my imagination,* I told myself.

I plopped down across from Dave at the Galaga machine. He was killing cartoon space bugs at an alarming rate. "How 'bout letting me play?"

"You're too drunk," he said not looking up, bashing buttons. Electronic death.

I thought about breaking into the jukebox the same way Dave had broken into the video game. I'd already done it dozens of times, replacing the more noxious songs with punk singles. Hated Youth, Roach Motel, Voodoo Idols, Street Kidz, the Panics and Lethal Yellow replaced Phil Collins, Michael Jackson, Tommy Tutone, the Oak Ridge Boys, REO Speedwagon and Kenny Rogers. The top forty shit went to the inside floor of the machine after spending some time Frisbee-skipping across the parking lot.

I picked up the fliers, and dropped them on the floor, then fell over loudly when I tried to pick them back up. I struggled back to my feet—Dave laughing and killing space bugs—kicked the pliers toward the kitchen and stumbled back into the dining area.

At the salad bar I steadied myself, almost vomiting onto the sneeze guard above the macaroni salad. I peered toward my destination and caught sight of Sissy in a clinch with Albino. Their eyes were closed. Albino blindly felt around for the zipper on Sissy's smock. Her hand gently fended him off. Pink-chipped, chewed-on fingernails. What should I do?

I should kick his ass, man.

I headed over, and was chopped mid-thigh by a table and flipped over it Dick Van Dyke-style, flopping pitifully onto the floor. "You're a mess," Sissy said, crouching over me. "You grab the other side."

Albino and Sissy half-dragged me out the door into the fresh air. "Gonna have to kick your ass, man," I said.

"Sure," Albino said. "Next time you're straight."

"Seriously, man."

"I know," he said. "Your keys in your pocket?"

"Jingle, jingle," I said.

We stopped at my van. Sissy fished the keys out, unlocked the sliding door and the two of them heave-hoed me in. "Don't worry about him," I heard her say after the door slid shut. "But still. Let's keep this more or less ..."

"Sure," Albino interrupted.

Silence.

"I've got to get him home," Sissy said. "We're probably in trouble enough already."

"Yeah," Albino said. "Later."

Sissy got in and adjusted the front seat so she could

reach the pedals. She popped a cigarette in her mouth and pushed in the cigarette lighter. "You're more trouble than you're worth," she said, unlit cigarette bobbing. She smiled back at me all sprawled out on the shag carpeting I'd stolen from a construction site last summer and installed using a hot glue gun. She plucked the cigarette out, held it in her fingers. "You think you can manage getting into the house? Otherwise I'll leave you to sleep it off in the van."

"I'll manage," I said.

"Jesus," she said, cranking the van into gear and backing out of the parking space. The van jerked forward. She'd stalled it. Three on the tree standard transmission. The engine started again. We rolled forward. "I'm only fifteen and I'm already sick to death of men." The lighter popped out and she lit her cigarette.

Hot Cars

Dave said he knew these two girls. Dave said they would definitely put out, no problem. Dave said a lot of things.

"Fuck you," I whisper-hissed into the kitchen phone. My mother might hear me. She was very Catholic.

"Don't be like that," Dave said.

"Fuck you very much," I said a little louder, peering around the corner, all twitchy and shit. The old lady was in the other room, kicked back and drinking a beer with her beige hosiery feet up on the ottoman, relaxing after a hard day of selling china to rich people down at Maas Brothers. The TV was on, and Merv Griffin was singing "Girl from Ipanema." "I remember the last time."

"Hey man," Dave said. "Don't even think about that. I'm still kind of pissed off."

"That makes two of us," I said. "What about Albino? Why can't he pitch in?"

"I'm throwing you this bone first, my man," he had the gall to say.

"Fuck you with a crowbar," I went, getting bored

24

with the conversation.

"How about if I front you ten bucks?" he said.

"Now I'm fucking listening," I said. Dave had set up the last blind date I'd been on. The chain of events started when his old lady sent him to a Christian retreat. She'd decided that he was doing too many drugs, even though he stole half his stash from her. It's a teenager's lot in life to put up with shit like that. So he went on this holy roller retreat and ended up in faith counseling with these three born-again girls who were not only sisters, they were identical triplets named Faith, Hope and Charity. One night at the Pizza Hut, I was helping him scrub out some pans in between the dinner rush and the late rush—I was the cook and Dave was the dish machine operator—and he blurts out his idea for a triple date involving these girls, him, me and Albino. It was decided that I would drive because I owned a Chevy van that could accommodate all the horny teens.

What is it about twins and triplets that fascinates guys so much?

So the next night, a Thursday, the only night we all had off, I drove Dave and Albino out into the boonies to pick up these supposedly hot chicks. They lived in a neighborhood with no name, on a street with no street sign and no blacktop. It was only a lane and a half of gravel and dirt.

Dead center in the weedy yard in front of their house

was a knee-high plastic Jesus that lit up from the inside, gazing up to heaven with a quizzical expression on His face. The hands reaching above His head completed the why-me look. A white extension cord snaked from Jesus' back into the house through a front window that wasn't completely shut.

The three of us walked along the festively colored, circular popcorn stones to the screened-in front door. It had a Jesus fish glued to it, which was starting to come unglued and slipping a bit in the heat.

"Praise the Lord," I said to Dave.

"Man, you don't want to start with your shit. Not if you want to score, motherfucker." He pressed the doorbell button. I was expecting it to play "Amazing Grace." It merely went ding-dong.

"Best behavior," Dave whispered, hand bladed to his peach fuzz rimmed mouth. "Especially you, Buzz." He glared at me. I shrugged it off and looked away.

"You must be the dates," this ugly, gap-toothed makeover mom said through the screen door.

I nudged Albino in the ribs. He shook his head in assent and shrugged. We'd silently agreed that when the mom is ugly, there's probably no hope for the daughters. And a second later, our hypothesis was confirmed.

Out they came, these girls, holy cats! They all wore Kmart blue light special dresses composed of stiff yellowish polyester accented with blood red stripes.

Blue, plastic old lady frames around coke bottle lenses slid down identical pug noses. The yellow in the dresses really accentuated their piss-colored hair and the stripes brought out the acne scars accented with red puss. The blue in the frames highlighted the tiny blue veins street mapped all over their exposed skin. They wore patent leather Mary Jane shoes. And one of them probably outweighed the three of us.

As soon as they emerged from the house, the inner door shut behind them. So much for Christian hospitality.

We loaded the three tubs in the van. One sat up front with me, while the other two climbed into the rear, onto the shag carpeting. They sat all prim and Indian-style, like they were something special. I popped a compilation tape I'd made into the cassette player I'd hot-glued to the dash. The cassette player was fed electricity through the cigarette lighter. Lethal Yellow howled out "The Obnoxious Song."

"Don't you have something different we could listen to?" the girl sitting next to Dave asked. I tilted my rearview so I could look down at them. Dave was not holding her in any way. Their knees weren't even touching. Score my ass.

"No," I said.

"What about the radio?" the one sitting near, but not touching Albino, asked.

I clunked off the cassette player and left the van in

silence for the duration, until we pulled the van into the bowling alley parking lot. Dennis, the guy who worked behind the counter most nights, didn't card you, which made it a popular hangout.

"Bowling?" my date sniffed.

"What's wrong with bowling?" I went.

"Nothing. We just expected … " and she looked back at her sisters for some help. They stared blankly at her. So much for triplet telepathy.

I parked and hopped out. I sniffed the palm of my hand. Pepperoni and onions. I slammed my door shut and started walking toward the place. A prick I knew from school was out front, all preppied up in a pink golf shirt and chinos. My jeans had tears in the knees, my Converse All Stars were worn through and the black pocket tee shirt I had on looked like someone had blasted it with a shotgun. It had been three or four months since my last haircut and I didn't own a comb.

"Hey!" one of the fat girls shouted. My date. "Ain't you gonna get the door like a gentleman?" She was hanging outside the open van door, her cottage cheese legs stretching toward the ground. Dave and Albino had already unassed their tubs from my rolling wreck. Dave slid the van door shut and helped my beast from her perch.

"Look, it's Pepper," said the pink-shirted prick. A couple more pink-shirted pricks came over. "Look who he's with." Snickering all around. I went to a Catholic high school that my family couldn't afford. It was the only private school in the area, and it attracted rich Protestant fuckheads who put their fuckhead kids through at twice the tuition price they charged for Catholics. "Hey, Pepper," shouted the pink prick, "shouldn't you be at work?" More snickering. They didn't believe in work. They believed in inheritance.

We pushed through the front doors of the bowling alley without saying a word. Things were bad enough without getting into a fight. Inside, we sat down at a semicircular booth like a bunch of Rat Packers. I was sent after the beer. Dennis wasn't there. Instead it was some anal dude wearing a personalized bowling shirt, who decided that my fake ID didn't pass inspection. "Nice try," the snotty fuck commented. I brought back some cokes on a serving tray. "Dennis isn't here," I said lamely. *"Reunited and it feels so gooood,"* came pumping out of the overhead speakers.

"Ain't we gonna get a lane?" Albino's date asked.

"If you're gonna dress identically, the least you could do is wear nametags," I said, patting myself for cigarettes and finding none while Albino and Dave exchanged this look which said, "now the fun begins." At that moment, I understood instantly what this whole "date" was about. This wasn't a real date. This was "let's get Pepper pissed off and watch him rip on the fat Christian chicks." And now I really was pissed off. "You dicks," I said.

"Excuse you?" Dave's date said.

"I wasn't talking to you, Jesus girl," I snapped, glaring at her.

"You'll have to forgive Buzz," Dave said, a smirk curling up and making itself at home on his bony face. "He hasn't been saved."

Albino pretended he was coughing into his fist. "And he's a Catholic," he gasped out.

My date grasped my arm and started jabbering, but I couldn't make most of it out through the blood roaring in my ears and the teeth grinding in my head. A set-up! These Bible pounders got extra points for nailing Catholics. My pals had set the lions on me. Of all the rotten, fucked-up things to do.

" ... because the Lord Jesus can be merciful ... "

"Merciful?" I roared. "Merciful? How the fuck can He be merciful when He's created a hideous chick like you. In triplicate?"

That shut her up. Her hands slipped off my arm. Albino and Dave were both cough-laughing into their fists.

I slid out of the booth. "I gotta take a whiz," I said, and stomped right out the front door and made a beeline to my van, whose rear tires had been flattened by the pink-shirted fascists. They'd done it before. They didn't have the nerve to actually slash the tires, or cut off the valve stems, so I kept a bicycle pump in the back of my van next to the spare tire. In no time, I had the van looking a lot less like it was humping the ground and drove it gingerly over to the Gulf station just up the street. A few clang-clang-clangs later and I was ready to go home.

When I got there, Sissy told me that Dave and Albino had called, all apologetic, but still laughing. "So, you going back to pick them up?" she asked.

"Would you?"

She laughed. A moment later we both were laughing.

Our brother Sparky, away at college, had left his collection of Susie B dollars in a drawer. He was sure that they would be valuable some day. We stole them and drove out to St. Armand's Key and had éclairs and coffee. Then we walked down to the North Lido Beach pavilion and made fun of the Euro tourists wearing their Speedos. So the evening wasn't a complete loss.

Back to the phone conversation.

"... I swear to you on my dad's stack of porno magazines ..."

"Your dad's stack of porno magazines," I said, interrupting him. "Put your money where your mouth is. I want five. Good ones," I said. "Not *Playboy*. I want *Hustler*."

"Five? I don't know if I can get away with five," Dave whined.

"Five," I said. "I'm very definite on five. Ten dollars and five porno mags rents you one *me* for the night."

"Deal," Dave went. It was too easy. "You'll see. We'll have a decent time. It's all copasetic."

"It better be." I hung up. I was to meet him at work in an hour.

Mom was slouched over, swigging a Manhattan. "That was work," I said. "Gotta go in."

"Yeah," Mom said. "See you." She sipped as Merv eww-ed at Elke Sommer. She was pretty hot for an old German chick.

I went into my room and put on a good pocket tee shirt and found a pair of All Stars that weren't sieved up. Then I went into the bathroom and attempted to comb my hair with Sissy's comb. I ran it partway through a couple of times, until it got stuck on knots and I gave up. Slipping down the hall to the master bath, I found my father's stash of Hai Karate. Slap, slap and I was ready for love.

My mother smelled me when I walked by. "Your father's cologne?"

"I put it on my hands, see," showing her my hands. "Trying to get rid of the pizza stink in advance."

"You and your sister," Mom noted. She swigged, then crunched down an ice cube as Merv showed off the lining of his coat before introducing Zsa-Zsa Gabor.

On the drive down, a nervous streak tickled through me. The feeling was like the time I did bennies with Albino after he'd stolen them from his fat mom. I giggled a bit and rolled down the window, spitting my Juicy Fruit onto the yellow line bisecting the road. "John Wayne was a Nazi," my cassette deck told me. "He liked to play SS." I asked myself, "Jesus, what the fuck?" It wasn't like I'd never been on a date before.

I passed the Publix, the porno shop, the 7-Eleven. I passed Tom's Gun Shop, Scottie's Lumber, and thump-thumped over the railroad tracks. Stop, look, listen. I pulled in and parked near the dumpster, like always, right over my personal oil stain. "Copasetic," I said.

Inside, the place was empty. Sissy, rolling silverware into paper napkins, waved me over to the table she was sitting at. Albino shouted, "Hey, man." He rotated a couple of pizzas in the gas-fired oven. I gave him a nod as I sat across from Sissy.

"I'm working tonight."

"You are?"

"Not really. Just if Mom asks."

"She won't."

"I'm going on a double-date with Dave."

"Anybody I know?"

"I don't even know her."

She finished rolling a set and reached over and smacked me on the head. "Dummy."

"That's me, all right."

"You look a little high."

"I'm straight. I don't know what the hell's going on."

"You're a dope. That's what's going on."

I took her cigarette out of the ashtray and took a long drag. It was a Merit, crap, like trying to suck smoke through fifty feet of garden hose. "Jesus," I said. "What do you get out of these things?"

She smiled. "I'm trying to cut down."

"Mission accomplished."

"There's Dave," she said, nodding at the door.

He strode over quickly, wearing a cowboy shirt with pearl buttons and a belt buckle the size of a dinner plate advertising the Arcadia rodeo. "Howdy, Jethro," I said, stubbing out the tasteless little cig.

"Fuck you," Dave replied, smiling.

"My ten bucks? My porno mags?"

"In my car," he said. "Glad to see you pressed a fresh tee shirt for tonight's adventure."

"Porno mags," Sissy muttered, shaking her head. She lit a new Merit, placed it in the ashtray and began rolling silverware again.

Dave reached over for the fresh smoke. "Don't bother," I said. "You'd be better off huffing library paste."

"C'mon," Dave said, giving up on the cig. "I wanna talk with you." We went through the kitchen and out the back door to the break area. Albino was out there zoning out, his head tilted back, eyes closed, his smock zipped open a bit so we could see his hollow chest. The print shop next door gave off petroleum fumes.

"Hands off Debbie," Dave said. "She's mine. I think I'm finally gonna do it with her. Not tonight, but maybe this weekend? So don't go blowing this thing. All you gotta do is be nice to her friend. Betty. Betty's pretty hot. At least that's Debbie's story."

"Fuck," I said.

"None of that. None of that fuck stuff, okay? We're gonna be riding with her dad over to this birthday party. So you gotta be ... Are you straight?"

"Yeah, I'm straight," I said, irritated.

"Because her dad's a cop. He's got a sixth sense about that kind of shit."

"So what about her dad?"

"He's driving," Dave said. "Aren't you listening to me?"

"Fuck yeah. Dad's a cop, no pot smoking. Right?"

"And you gotta smile. Jesus, man. You always look like somebody just killed your dog. Try to look happy, fuckface."

"How's this?" I asked, putting on a shiteater of a grin.

"I knew I shouldn't have called you. You better not ruin this for me. I figured I owed you after last time." He felt around himself for smokes and realized he'd left them somewhere else.

"What about me?" Albino asked.

"What about you?" Dave snapped.

"I'm the one who had to call my old man after Buzz split. How fucked up is that?" He hadn't moved, hadn't opened his eyes. "Either of you guys have a smoke? I'm all out."

"Me, too," I said.

"Me, three," Dave said. "Smile, Pepper. Okay, Jesus, at least try to look less unhappy."

A horn tooted in the parking lot and we all trotted around the corner. When we got within sight of the car, a shitty Vega, we slowed to a strut, jammed hands in pockets, trying to look all cool.

A smiling brunette and a black-haired girl with angry eyes were in the backseat, kind of gigglesome. Dave scooted in and sat beside them after dad hopped out and peeled his seat forward. I sat in the empty front seat beside dad, who immediately snapped in a Beach Boys eight-track. *"Help me Rhonda yeah."*

Dave said, "This is Debbie." Debbie was the smiling brunette. She jerked her hand toward me. I contorted around and shook the bony, cold thing. "And this is Betty, I guess."

"Yeah, I'm Betty," Betty said. She narrowed her eyes at Dave.

I poked my head above the seat and smiled at her. "Hi," I said.

"Fasten your seatbelt," Dad said. He thumped the

bumper sticker adhesed to the glove compartment, which said FASTEN YOUR SEATBELT. SEATBELTS SAVE LIVES. I clicked mine in place just as we hit the street full bore, doing 80 in a 45 zone without a care in the world. "What do you think?" Dad asked me.

"Um, she seems very nice," I said.

"About the car, junior," Dad said.

"It looks like a piece of crap, but it isn't," I said.

It was the right thing to say. Dad smiled at me. "You get it, then." And then he downshifted and went even faster. We flew over the railroad tracks. Bee Ridge Road was a blur.

"Betty's Italian," Dave said.

"Greek!" she went.

"Say something in Italian," Dave said.

"Greek!" she went.

"We're going to an Italian birthday party," Dave said.

"Greek," she said, her voice tiring.

It was an old game. They obviously knew each other from sometime before. Anyone could tell. I turned and peered over at Dave as Sarasota whizzed past. He was staring past Debbie, his date, over at the girl he'd claimed he'd found for me. Hunger.

"How do you know Dave?" Dad asked me.

"We work together," I said. The engine roared as we went over the Stickney Point Bridge, onto Siesta Key. Whoever these Greeks or Italians were, they had money.

The bridge buzzed under us. Dad braked quickly, jerking us all forward. We went through a light, and pulled into the parking lot for Turtle Beach.

A band played under a gazebo. People danced and sang. I jerked forward in my seat, realized I was belted in, unbelted, and got out of the car. Betty shouted, "They're singing '*Xronia Polla*'! Hurry!" She ran over while the rest of us followed at a slower pace.

On the table under the little roof were several clear bottles of Ouzo. I filled a Dixie cup and splashed in some punch for color. The song was finished and everyone all clapped, then grabbed metal forks out of a pile and dug into the white (with a blue flag) cake, a cheese pie, a spinach pie, and several baklavas. There weren't any plates; you were supposed to reach in with the fork and grab whatever you could. I tried a bite of everything. Then I belted down the Ouzo and got such a head rush that I almost fell over. I had another. And one more for good measure. I looked around and saw that everyone was talking and laughing and having a great time, all these Greeks, but all I could hear were the waves lapping the shore, a seagull calling out, my own breathing. The rest was silence. "Ouzo," I said, experimentally. The word sounded distant and fucked up. I walked several yards and sat down on a seagull-shit-covered bench with my dirty fork in one hand and the near-empty paper cup in the other. I had one more bite of baklava on the tines of my fork. I put it in my mouth. Chew, chew.

Debbie came over and sat next to me. "He doesn't really like me," she said. She was a ragged thing, her hair cheaply dyed, press-on nails slipping off, runs in her stockings, a stain on her dress. "Quit looking at me like that," she said, depressed. I turned my gaze back toward the party. The sound was still muted; all I could hear was the surf and the gulls. And Debbie. "He's using me," she said. I swallowed the baklava, and couldn't remember what it tasted like seconds later. "He really likes Betty." Her makeup was streaking down her face.

"Your life's like mine," I said, meaning it and not meaning it, not knowing why I said it. I wasn't trying to get laid. Maybe pity made those words come out.

"Your life sucks," Debbie said, pulling herself up and slumping back over to the party.

I flipped my fork. It tumbled end over end and stuck into the sugar white sand. I finished off the dribble of Ouzo and dropped the cup, pulled off my sneakers and socks, my tee shirt. No one was watching me. They were all having a good time. I dropped my trousers and stepped out of them. All that separated me from nudity were my white cotton briefs, which I left on.

I ran toward the surf, past an old man with a metal

detector, and belly-flopped in. First one stroke then another, until I caught a rhythm and headed out to sea. There was nothing but my arms and legs and the warm, salty gulf.

I wondered when I'd stop.

Holiday in Sarasota

I have always had a need for certain people to hate me. And if those people don't hate me, I feel like a failure. It's sort of an affirmation of what I am not.

For instance, this giggly waitress named Bunni. She dotted the 'i' with a smiley face, or sometimes a heart, on the customers' checks. That should tell you all you need to know about Bunni.

Even though it would be a week before my paycheck showed it, the time and a half I got for working Christmas Eve felt like an early Christmas present. There were only four of us working that night: me, Janet, Albino and Bunni. Sissy was at home with our goddamned family. She had tried to get on shift, but had spurned Janet's advances more than once and was now on her shit list. No time and a half for little sister.

Janet had transferred her crush to Bunni, who was unaware of it. Bunni was unaware of most things outside of her boyfriend, Chad, the quarterback of the Riverview Rams High School football team. Chad, Chad, Chad!

Chad was dreamy and brutal, blond and kickass. High school quarterbacks peak in high school and it's all they can think about years later while their beating their wife and children, holding down a shitty job in sales and thinking that they're better than sales, better than the pathetic non-quarterback family they're stuck with. I knew all about this. My father was a high school quarterback.

A pair of teens walked in and asked, "Are you open?" I was standing there in uniform, leaning against the make table, my arms crossed. I turned my head. "Customers!"

Nothing.

"Go sit down," I said. "I'll find the waitress." They just stood there. Obviously, they didn't take direction well. They both had feathered hair and flawless tanned skin, pretty open mouths and white teeth, and those unreadable blank eyes. They'd both go far in life. This criminal country is built for people like that. "Me find waitress," I said, shooing them to a table. "You sit."

"Puh," went the boy, attempting condescension. It flew past me into outer space with all those episodes of *I Love Lucy*. They finally glided into the empty dining area.

I tromped into the back. Albino was leaning against the tubular metal shelving filled with all the gigantic cans of chickpeas, pineapple chunks, mushrooms and black olives. He was sucking on a Kool, staring at Bunni, who was curled up on the prep table reading that fuckass book, *The Hobbit*. I hated Tolkien. All he wrote was ponderous escapist bullshit that bore no resemblance to real life. Evil is too evil to be actually evil. And good is impossibly good. And it's written like a high school history textbook, so that the dicks that read it can pat themselves on the back for being smart.

"Look at her," Albino said. "She's fun to look at, but you know she'd be no good in the sack. She'd just lay there, asking you if you're done yet."

I plucked the Kool from his fingers and took a nice draw.

"Keep it," he said.

I tapped some ashes on the clean tile floor. I walked over to Bunni and shook her shoe. "Hey, dipshit."

"Huh?"

"Customers," I said.

"My name's not dipshit," she said, and fucking giggled. Christ. "My name's Bunni."

"That's not a name," I replied. "It's a life sentence." I flicked the butt at the Hobart in the corner. Its barrel still had gooey crust glopped along the inside from when I had made the evening's batch of thin-and-crispy dough. "Let's see a little life."

She swung her feet and slapped them on the floor, and walked away pretending to be angry. Pretending! Before she turned the corner into the dining area, she stopped and aimed a big mock frown at me, lower lip a-bulge.

I flipped her off. What else was I supposed to do? Then I walked back out front to the ovens. Janet, a brutal-looking little woman, came wandering in. She was only thirty-nine, but seemed a lot older. "After this customer, we'll take off," she said. A white-ridged scar ran from her upper lip to the side of her nose. I imagined that she'd bitten through an Archie and Veronica jelly jar glass.

"Why don't we chase those two out now?" I asked as Bunni came sauntering up with her red-and-white ticket book and peeled off the order. A small, thin-and-crispy with pepperoni. Each "i" was dotted with a smiley face. "Order up," she said. "They tried to order beer, but I'm like 'no way.'"

"We're having a party over at my apartment," Janet said. "You're all invited. Very cozy."

"Um, I'd need a ride," Bunni said.

"You can ride with me," Janet said.

"Could you give me a ride?" Bunni asked me.

I could have made a sexual crack, but I didn't. "Albino's driving."

"I'll ask him," she said, and skipped away, the little bells in her shoelaces jingling.

"Great," I said to Janet. "Fucking swell."

"I don't know why you don't like her," Janet said. "She's a hot number."

"She's an asshole," I said. "Let's just leave it at that." I reached into the Rubbermaid garbage can and pulled a hunk off of the 25-pound dough ball. I worked the blob a bit, clunked on the dough flattener, which rumbled and spun stainless steel rollers like something out of *Mad Max*, and ran the blob through the top part, where it became an oval, then through the bottom, where it became a circle. I flopped it onto a small thin-and-crispy pan, used a rolling pin to cut off the excess along the top, then ran the spiky roller across the dough circle to perforate it so it wouldn't bubble up in the oven. I ladled on some sauce, swirled it even, sprinkled on the cheese, tossed on a few pepperoni slices, shook on the fairy dust (oregano and parmesan mixed together in a shaker) and slid the mess into the gas-fired oven atop one of the hot spots so it would cook faster.

"It's sad how quickly you can do that," Janet said.

"I'm a robot," I said. Then smiled. "Just like Reagan." The joke going around at the time was that Reagan had been created by Disney World for the Hall of Presidents and was merely out on loan to the government.

"Don't joke about the commander-in-chief," she said, and was serious about it. Even though she was a lesbian, and Reagan's uptight boy Meese would have her put in a reeducation camp in western Nebraska with dogs and searchlights and rubber hoses if he could have gotten away with it, she was also a Vietnam veteran, and had been almost blown up in a nightclub in Saigon. Hence the patriotism.

She was about to give me another one of her Americanism lectures, but then she remembered it was Christmas, I guess, and decided to let me off the hook. She instead went to the dish machine area to harass Albino. For the past week, she'd wanted to show him a mole on her back and every time she made like she was going to do it—turn her back toward him and peel off her top—he would freak out. This pleased her greatly.

The pizza was mostly burned when I pulled it out of the oven, but who gives a fuck, right? I let the cheese cure for a minute, then cut it up and slid it onto an aluminum serving tray, and under the heat lamp it went. I pushed Bunni's number, and rang the little doorbell for her to come get the pizza. Then I ducked into the back and found the butt I'd flicked at the dough mixer. I lit it back up and took that last, luxurious drag before tossing it back where I had found it. I thought, for a moment, about cleaning the dough barrel. Instead, I draped a discarded apron from the laundry bag over it.

Janet came back and sat at the little desk where she did the books. "I made those kids pay," she said. "Register's closed. I'm going to go make the drop. Clean up and head on over." She spiraled the store key off her key ring. "You lock up." She smirked at me. "Have a nice ride over with Bunni."

After chasing the two preppies out, we all helped ourselves to beer out of the tap. Albino peeled up the grate beneath the tap and showed Bunni the yeast monster clogging the drain, where the drip-drops of excess beer went to die. Lots of squealing and hopping up and down. Yawn. Grossing her out was as easy as punting a Chihuahua.

In the car, Albino made to change the station. "No wait," I said.

"Don't tell me you *like* this corny old song," Albino sneered. He was frozen in place, palming the steering wheel with one hand and reaching toward the quadraphonic with the other.

"I like it," Bunni said.

"Shut the fuck up, Bunni," we both went.

"Just listen. There's a great line in there," I said.

"Fuck you."

"No listen. Here it comes," I said.

We listened. The line came.

"I clean my gun … "

" ' … and dream of Galveston,'" I sang, completing it.

"Did he just say that?" Albino asked. A smile across pink lips. A twinkle across streetlamp-glittered eyes. "I have a whole new appreciation for Glen Campbell."

"Murder-suicide rarely finds its way into the top 40,"

I said.

"Suicide?" Bunni asked.

"Sure. Isn't that the way it always happens? They off the girlfriend, then blow themselves away? Besides, he sings 'before I die' or some shit."

"That's gross," Bunni said.

"Shut the fuck up, Bunni," we both went.

Sarasota looked particularly shitty that night. It was empty, as the January snowbirds with their Ohio plates and fucked-up driving and loudmouthed insistence on non-rude behavior had yet to descend. "You want friendly service? Take I-75 north." I could say shit like that because I was young in an old place that needed young people. Who else was going to dust their pizza with Bon Ami, or piss in their spaghetti water? It sure as hell wasn't going to be another sneering old coot. They were all retired, and wanted their lawns to be cut, their food to be prepared, their highballs to be delivered in a timely manner. And there was nobody but us sneaky teenaged natives to do it for them.

A lone mercury-vapor lamp provided a dull glow over the Corona Courtyard Apartments parking lot. Most of the spaces were marked with apartment numbers, and were unoccupied. Albino coasted the Cougar into a visitor's spot—we being good citizens—turned the ignition off, and yanked the emergency brake. He had been over to the boss' place before. Her girlfriend, Cindy, dealt primo pot, and rolled fat joints and only charged a buck for two. She was the best dealer in the world. That's the real reason he came over. The reason I came over was a little more complex. It had to do with my fucked up crush on Cindy.

We walked to the door, all identically dressed in red smocks and floppy red hats. Albino and I had dinner-plate-sized stains over our abdomens. I knocked on the door. It was a hollow-core with three gold-and-black, adhesive-backed ones pasted on it. This would make everything easier when the superheroes from the sheriff's department came by to kick it and make some arrests for the benefit of the *Sarasota Herald-Tribune*.

"Hey," we all said to each other when the door cracked open. Cindy was luscious-creamy baby fat skin and long curly hair. She had a hurt, Marilyn Monroe thing going, was in her mid-20's, with drowsy eyes. You'd never guess she was lesbo, or that she was Janet's mate. She opened the door wide and rushed us all in, and, as she was quadruple securing it with a slide bolt and chain, deadbolt and knob lock, she gave me this long, steamy look. I probably imagined it, I told myself, swallowing hard, dick stiffening.

Cindy took Bunni by the elbow and led her away for some girl talk, leaving us with free roam of the apartment. Albino took off for the kitchen, where the rolling operation took place. I announced to no one in particular that I needed to take a leak.

It was a two-bedroom, like they were trying to fool somebody. I slipped into the master bath unseen. A mirror in there covered the entire north wall so I could watch myself piss, then watch myself wash my hands, then watch myself rummage though the medicine cabinet. Bingo! The VA had given Janet a script for Valium. I popped two right away from the brown bottle, then took two—*no three!*—extras and slipped them into the penny pouch of my wallet. Then I turned on the tap and slowly swung shut the little medicine cabinet door, closing it soundlessly. I sucked water out of cupped hands and splashed my face, wiping off on a soft orange towel with duckies sewn on it.

I found myself full of longing. Full of despair. Then a ruthless tranquility. Then I was sitting on the edge of the bed, watching a 13-inch black-and-white Magnavox. A rerun of an old Bing Crosby Christmas Special? No it's Perry Como? The local news? "Buzz," a familiar voice went. "Buzz!" it insisted. "Have you been back here the whole time?"

"What whole time?"

"We've been here for two hours," it said.

"Shit, I'm supposed to be opening Christmas presents," I said, kind of snapping out of it.

"You gotta see this," Albino whispered. "Be very quiet."

I got up and tiptoed down the little hallway. At the end, the living room. A couch, an easy chair. "Clarence!" Jimmy Stewart shouted from the TV. Janet sat on the easy chair, the back of her head to us. On the couch, a miracle, like the second coming. On the couch, Cindy and Bunni making out, shirtless, bra-straps unshouldered, their tongues probing the insides of each other's cheeks. When I got my breath back, I whispered, "How?"

"We were passing around joints. I don't know. I ate a pan of brownies. I got up from the kitchen and there you have it," Albino said.

Janet turned and looked over at us, contented as a banker. She hoisted herself up and came over. "Time for you two to leave," she said, slipping Albino a twenty.

"You never know," I said, still watching.

"Know?" Janet asked.

"People," I said.

"Get out of here," Janet said, smiling gently. "Say hi to your sister for me."

"Sure," I said, and a mini-surge of anger passed through me, then winked away. I should have stolen all her Valium.

She crept back over to her chair. Albino sneaked in the kitchen and swiped a bottle of Dago red. He yanked my sleeve. I looked at him dumbly. "C'mon," he said. I took the restaurant key out of my pocket and flipped it onto the carpeting.

We passed the bottle back and forth all the way back to the Pizza Hut. When we got there, I opened the door to get out of the car.

"Bunni," I said. "And Cindy."

"I know," Albino said. "That was … " His mouth hung open. There were no words for it.

"Yeah," I said. I slammed the door shut.

I drove my van home slowly, deliberately, exactingly. I pulled up onto the front yard and parked on a sapling that had never grown into anything like a tree. I heard it snap under my front tire.

I had weird dreams where it was Sissy, and not Bunni, on the couch with Cindy. Or that it was Sissy and Bunni. I woke up the next morning, my sister shaking my foot. My mouth tasted funny. "Mom's cleaning up your mess in the bathroom," she said.

"Cleaning?" I went.

"Yeah. It's like a vomit explosion in there," she said. She was snapping fingers with one hand then popping the resulting hollowed fist into the palm of the other. "She's mad. She says you ruined Christmas."

"Sorry," I said.

"Sorry probably won't cut it," Sissy said. She seemed

very pleased with me. She had the same satisfied look on her face as when she had knelt on my arms and thumb-popped my forehead zits.

I rolled over a bit, reached into my pocket and dug out my wallet. "Hair of the dog," I said, dry-swallowing a Valium.

Sissy sat down next to me on the twin bed, feet dangling. She placed her hand over my heart, her eyes half-lidded, and smiled. "Good times," she said.

Institutionalized

Dave's mom had gone too far this time, and now he needed to be rescued. She'd had him locked up in Clearwater at this evangelical drying-out center. They wouldn't let him pee most of the time and when they did, he had to be escorted. They harangued him on papists, Jews and idolaters of all stripes, saying that they were the reason he had fallen into a life of drinking and drugs. They made him confess his sins and sing church hymns. We knew this because it was all recorded and mailed home on cassette tapes slipped into tacky Bible-quoting cardboard sleeves.

He'd been gone a week before I'd noticed that he hadn't been at work, and that I hadn't seen him at our usual haunts. I wasn't much of a friend, I guess.

It was Sissy who decided we'd bust him out of there, *Mission Impossible*-style, maybe going through the cooling vents, or up and down elevator shafts, or dressed as guards. We'd slap kiwi black on our faces and do karate moves. *Hi-ya!*

Sissy thought this all up while she and I were at *A Long Night at Camp Blood*, a slasher movie that featured a gaggle of very annoying kids getting hacked to pieces by an agile, machete-twirling corpse. We'd seen it twice before. I liked the music, which was mostly early 70's metal tunes. Sissy liked cheering on the killer, who wore a bloody flour sack over his head and wheezed pitifully. We talked loudly through the picture, mocking it and reveling in it at the same time.

"Why's he all dirty?" I asked.

"Because he's been buried," Sissy replied.

"Uh, why's he wheeze so much?"

"Because he's been *buried*. Don't you listen? He's got dust and chinch bugs in his lungs." Then she shouted, "Kill him! Not *him*, the other moron! He always kills the wrong guy first." *A Long Night at Camp Blood* eventually spawned 13 sequels—*Camp Blood II, Camp Blood III in 3D, Camp Blood: The Final Chapter, Camp Blood: The Revenge of Mother, Camp Blood: The Horror Continues*, and on and on.

Sissy said—as the killer got clanged on the head with a cast-iron skillet by the girl who would be the lone survivor, but not until the killer had been dropped down a well, set on fire with a flaming arrow, blown up in a grain silo and blasted with a Civil War cannon that, oddly, had been left loaded for a hundred and twenty years—"We ought to bust Dave out," sparking her pink, daisy-appliquéd lighter to witness my reaction.

I nodded at her. "Sure," I said.

"You don't seem very certain of yourself," she said, letting the flame die.

"Why don't you kids shut up?" some fatass behind us asked.

Something blew up on screen. The killer. He'd been shot with that flaming arrow after climbing out of the well. The theater went orange and red. Sissy turned around and said, "You actually came to *watch* this piece of shit?"

The fat guy shifted his buttocks miserably in his seat and cut his eyes away.

A couple days later, we all chipped in for a case of beer, and Albino found a guy who knew a guy who would sell us a nickel bag of Gainesville Gold. I made a compilation tape for the trip up, which received the seal of approval when my old man came busting into my room and told me to turn that crap down, was that supposed to be music, blah, blah, blah.

We synchronized our watches in the Pizza Hut parking lot. It was 11:59 p.m., now 12:00 exactly, our shift was over. We'd changed into all-black clothing. Well, mostly all black as concert tee shirts were involved. And my beat-up Army jacket was olive drab. And, okay, our All Stars had white laces and white rubber edging.

Still, we were dressed in black in spirit, if not in fact. The guy who knew the guy asked us what we were up to.

"We're the last of the SLA. We're gonna go grab Patty Hearst. This time we know she'll stay with us 'cause we're super hardcore," Sissy said.

"No, shit?" the guy who knew the guy said.

"You're not too bright, are you?" Sissy said, and climbed into the passenger seat of the van.

"Hey," the guy who knew the guy said, offended a bit. But he was alone and Albino was waving him into the back of the van.

"Get in, dickhead," Sissy said.

I revved the engine.

The guy who knew the guy stumbled into the back, and the sliding door slid shut, thump.

"Hey, ho. Let's go," Albino said, and we did. We drove over to this shitty house up in Bradenton. B-town is a lot like Sarasota, except poorer and scarier. Albino and the guy went into the house A few minutes later, Albino emerged alone, hands in pockets, shrugging against the sudden cold. He climbed in the back and slammed the door shut. "Fuck *me*," he said. He pulled out a tiny sandwich bag with barely enough grass in it to make a joint. He waved it at us indignantly. "You call that a nickel bag? What the fuck's this world coming to?"

"Easy there, old timer," Sissy said. "Who brought the rolling papers?" We looked around at each other. "Start the van, Buzz. Let's get out of here before somebody steals our hubcaps. Somebody already stole our common sense."

I reached over and hit play on the cassette deck. It was empty. I'd forgotten the compilation tape. I fumbled around and found a tape and jammed it in there. It was Dave yowling, "Jesus loves me! This I know, for the Bible tells me so. Little ones to Him belong. They are weak, but He is strong … "

Sissy popped the tape out. "Depressing," she said. She turned on the AM radio instead. The cardboard mailer revealed Dave's new address. Sissy flicked on the map light and studied the Rand McNally. We found US 41, then discovered the road leading to the Sunshine Skyway Bridge, a scary, former two-span reduced by God's sense of humor to one span. The year before, a freighter had crashed into the Sunshine Skyway during a blinding spring storm. The middle of one of the two bridge spans that connected Bradenton with St. Petersburg tore apart and dropped into the bay. Something like fifty people plunged to their deaths, most of them destitute fuckers riding a Greyhound bus. Car after car after bus followed each other's taillights to death. I heard about it on my father's AM radio while on the way to my high school for a mandatory Catholic bullshit retreat. That's when they try to brainwash you into being a priest, or at the very least never enjoying sex in your life, ever.

My father gave me an angry look when I laughed. "You think that's funny?" he asked. He enjoyed getting mad, so it wasn't hard to rile him. He was not a Catholic. He was a Methodist. It wasn't a mixed marriage because he converted for my mother's sake. He didn't buy into all the guilt and repression, but let our mother dump it into our heads anyway.

"No, I don't think it was funny," I said. "I don't know why I laughed."

The fog was pretty thick, maybe ten feet of visibility. He tried to concentrate on the road, but was having a hard time. He didn't like to drive slowly.

"I laughed when I heard my father had died. No kidding," he said, all serious. "I didn't think it was funny, but I laughed." He wasn't good at being serious. He squinched up his face like he was thinking. He wasn't good at thinking. "You kinda react weird sometimes."

We had never met his father, or his mother either, as they both died before we were born. We didn't give too much thought to the missing grandparents because the rest of the Pepper family was so white-trashy that we considered it a blessing that we had two fewer Peppers to contend with. On the rare occasion that one of the Pepper relatives descended for a visit, we locked up the valuables, or hid them the best we could. Not that we had much that was of value.

It was the poor people on the bus. That's what had

gotten to me. I remembered seeing them when my other grandparents, not the dead ones, would come to visit. My grandfather didn't believe in flying. He thought it was unnatural to wing through the air in a metal tube. Plus he had a theory that air travel was some sort of capitalist plot to keep the working man down. As a result, my grandfather and grandmother always rode the bus with all the poor people, folks who were down to their last dimes and didn't know where they'd get the money to clothe the baby that was puking thin breast milk all over their raggedy shoulders. You could see it on their faces as they stepped bashfully off the bus, peering around for the cop that would arrest them. My grandparents always got off the bus last so that my mother, my sister, my brother and I could get a good look at the parade of human misery. Now those desperate faces flashed in my mind. They had gotten the final kick in the ass from Jesus. People on a Greyhound wonder if anything worse can happen to them. That morning, on a windswept bridge, Jesus let them know. I turned my head toward the window and tried not to cry, as my father would slug me if he saw me cry. He was old-fashioned that way.

I clicked off the AM radio halfway through "Bohemian Rhapsody." I paid the toll. I gulped, then gripped the steering wheel hard. I rolled my window shut. "Here we go," I said, shifting into second and leaving it there. The van's tires buzzed as we zipped over the top of the

Sunshine Skyway's remaining span. The other span still looked like someone had kicked the shit out of it. I only glanced over, but Sissy and Albino were fixated, ooohing and ahhhing over the devastation. I wondered if that bus was still down there.

Over the top and descending, I gasped out my relief. "Did you see any of that?" Albino asked me.

"I can't be rubbernecking, I have to drive," I said. "Hand me a beer, will you?" I shifted into third. It felt good.

"Oh shit," Albino said. "I almost forgot about the beer." He was performing surgery on a Winston, converting it for illegal use.

Beers were popped, warm by this time, and foamy. "Hey, this tastes like ... " I started.

"It's Red, White and Blue!" my sister shrieked. Our father's favorite brand!

"You guys didn't give me much money," Albino said.

"You're batting a thousand tonight, boy," Sissy growled. She whipped her can out the window.

"Maybe we can stop somewhere," I said, wincing and drinking. You'd think I'd be used to this donkey piss by now, having stolen it out of the fridge forever.

"No way. Not in Pinellas County," Albino said. "It's nothing but blue laws up here."

We didn't have any money left anyway.

I turned the radio back on. *We had joy we had fun we*

had seasons in the sun. Sissy growled, "I wish this guy would kill himself already." I was following I-275, but we wouldn't be able to do that for much longer, or else we'd end up on the Courtney Campbell Causeway heading nonstop to Tampa. Albino torched the makeshift joint. "Get off here," Sissy said, taking the joint from Albino. I took the next exit ramp and headed north along a four-lane highway with a weed-choked median.

We motored through the deserted streets of St. Petersburg, nary a car in sight, not even cops. Ragged palm trees and busted pavement, strip malls with storefronts for rent and supermarkets with signs that said, "We honor food stamps." Ford and Carter's hyperinflation and Reagan's recession had taken their toll.

"Turn left up here," Sissy said. I cranked open the window a little. We were close to the beach. You could smell the red tide.

We passed by it the first time, assuming that it was some kind of corporate headquarters. Eventually, I saw a sign featuring a golden cross that informed us that "Jesus Is Lord."

"That's gotta be it," I said.

"It doesn't look like any hospital I've ever seen," Albino said.

I drove a circle around it; the place took up an entire city block. The building was covered in smoked glass, which shined under the starry night. The outside was surrounded by neatly trimmed hedges. There was a break in the hedges, and a sidewalk cutting through, leading up to the building. I stopped the van there and got out. Sissy and Albino followed. I finished off my beer and dropped the empty in the gutter. A fighter jet burst through the sky above, shredding the sky, heading toward McDill Air Force Base.

We strode down the sidewalk to the building. There was no handle on the door, just a camera overhead aimed at where we stood. I glanced up at the camera, then cupped my hands over my face and tried to peek inside. I couldn't see a thing, not even my own reflection.

I banged a fist on the door. "The papist's here!" I shouted.

"The Jew's here!" Albino shouted.

"I guess that makes me the idolater," Sissy said.

A siren whirred, far off, but getting closer.

"Let's book," Albino said.

"We came this far," I said.

"Albino's right," Sissy said, pulling on my sleeve.

"What about Dave?" I asked.

"They can't keep him here forever," Albino said.

We ran for the van, giggling, our feet slapping the bleached concrete. We hopped in, I popped the emergency brake and the clutch, and away we went. We spun past a 7-Eleven, empty and gleaming, and down side streets, turning one way, then another, tires squealing, the van threatening to tip over. After about fifteen minutes of aimless driving, we realized we were lost.

I turned into an unnamed neighborhood and took my foot off the gas, slowing way down, downshifting. The houses we passed were pastel stucco, like fruity frosted birthday cakes, all identically formed. We cruised silently through the well-lit streets, looking for a way out, but all the side roads dead-ended into palmetto brush.

Sissy studied the map. I slowed down a couple times so she could read the street names. This neighborhood wasn't on the map. It didn't exist. There were no dogs yapping. No house lights on. No cabbage-sized weeds, or dead patches of grass. No rusted wrecks on cinderblocks. We rolled down the window, letting the cold night air keep us awake. There were no sounds. It was a mausoleum of the living. Little boats on trailers and Dodge Aspens to pull them. Curvy ceramic shingles. House numbers spray-stenciled on the curb. Mailboxes shaped like duckies and ponies. Postage stamp lawns. Sickly, tall, transplanted palm trees arching over the road. Street after street, long and straight, and as constricted as our throats. Shades drawn. The people inside all living voiceless lives, waiting for Jesus to take them to a similar place where they would remain this way forever. It was like looking into a future where someone slowly presses down on your face with a pillow until you suffocate, unnoticed. It made you want to be seventeen forever.

"The American dream," Albino said, trying to make a joke out of it.

I'm Not Your Stepping Stone

Janet's girlfriend Cindy had run off with Bunni, the underage waitress. The two of them were heading toward Massachusetts, because they'd heard that lesbians could get married nice and legal there. Bunni's parents had gotten the cops involved. Cindy was in big damn trouble.

"You warned me about that Bunni," Janet said. "You told me she was an asshole, but I didn't listen."

Sure, but that was before I saw her kissing Cindy. I didn't say that, though. I shook my head like I was agreeing with her. "I guess I should go back up front."

"Imagine having the nerve to do something like that," Janet fumed.

The nerve? My respect for Bunni had grown tremendously. A lesbian cheerleader dumping the head jock for a joint-rolling chick in her mid-20's. Now that takes some guts, especially in a shitty, Deep South town like Sarasota. But I didn't say that, either. Instead I snorted, and shook my head melancholically, like I was mourning the nation's youth. "So, I should get up front."

"To come into your own home ... "

I left Janet mid-sentence. I didn't have to give a shit about what she had to say anymore. After today, her reign was finito. She had found a new job as head chef at an old age home, slopping the geezers.

I poured myself a Mountain Dew from the to-go fountain, no ice, and drank it while leaning against the make table. No rules in these times of chaos and uncertainty. *Viva la revolucion.*

Chuck, the area supervisor, came in wearing a black vest, black hat and Pizza Hut shirt, instead of his usual Johnny Carson-like suit. The new getup meant that he was now the manager.

"What's going on, Chuck?" I asked, waving at his clothes while quickly hiding my red cup behind the dough flattener.

"I've been demoted. You know how long it took me to get out of this place?" Chuck had hired me and Sissy.

"Six years," I said.

"Six years," Chuck said. "Pizza Hut can kiss my ass."

"You've been saying that for a long time, Chuck," I said.

"Seven years," Chuck said. "But this time I mean it."

Nothing was happening, no orders were up, so I followed him to the back to hear what he would say to Janet. "You lucky asshole," he said to her. "I'd jump at the chance to get out of this racket."

"Lucky," Janet said. "Nice to have a word for it."

"Oh, yeah. Sorry about Cindy. I always liked her," Chuck said.

"Yeah, you and every man, woman, child and dog in this burg," Janet said. "*You* liked her too, didn't you?" She was talking to me.

"Sure," I said, trying to sound noncommittal. "Why not?"

"You had a cute, little crush on her. I could tell," Janet said, disgusted. "Even now you do. Look at you."

I crossed my arms and tried not to appear the way I felt, totally angry and burning.

Chuck leaned back against the wall next to where Janet was working, and tilted his head back. His eyes were red-rimmed, his mouth formed in a little oh, breathing in and out. A caged zoo animal. Poke him with a stick, feed him a peanut. I hoped, at that moment, that I would never feel the way Chuck looked.

Janet popped a tiny, blue pill and washed it down with some Pepsi—and probably a little something extra—from a red plastic glass. The VA was going to keep her hopped up for the rest of her life. America's way of saying thanks to its brave warriors.

"Anyway," Chuck said, wearily, "are you ready to turn over the books?"

The weeks and months passed by. The seasons changed from winter to spring. I got a D-minus in Moral Guidance, but did well enough in my other classes to make the honor roll. I popped zits in the mirror. Summer came, and I switched to the morning shift at the Pizza Hut, as did Sissy.

I opened the place at seven every morning. I had a routine. One day, I broke into the jukebox, pulled out "Bette Davis Eyes," and "My Sharona," winged them across the parking lot, then put them back in the jukebox. After that, the songs would pop-skip-end if anyone tried to play them. Another day, I broke into the Galaga machine and gave myself five quarters worth of playing time. Sissy sat at a table smoking a cigarette, taking a first thing in the morning break, since it only took her fifteen minutes to set up.

On page three of the Suncoast section, she saw it, and pointed it out to me. Cindy and Bunni had been arrested in Boston trying to scam a marriage certificate.

A week later, Cindy came walking through the door, in uniform. I watched her punch in, then pretended to be interested in the dough I was prepping. "How you doing, slugger?" she asked. She sat down on the prep table and watched me wrestle the dough out of the mixer.

"Fine," I said, grunting, jerking and hefting the blob of dough out and flopping it into the Rubbermaid garbage can. Thump. I placed the lid on it so the dough wouldn't dry up. "What're you doing here?" I asked her suspiciously, slapping my hands together.

"I didn't get married," she said, smiling. "Did you know that none of the fifty states allow gay marriages? Not even liberal Massachusetts?" She hopped down from the prep table, walked over to me and pinched a button on my chest. "What's this?" I could taste her breath. It was full of cinnamon toast. Tasting a woman's breath is the most erotic thing on earth.

"N-Nuke the Knack," I said, trying to control myself.

"The Knack?"

"A very bad band," I said, blinking erratically. "An evil band."

"Evil, eh?" She smiled evilly. Her lips were pink and puffy. Her eyes were crystal, blue-green oceans. I could see how carefully she applied her makeup. She licked her teeth, narrowed her eyes, smiled again and bit her lower lip.

I backed up quickly, building up some momentum, then flipped over the garbage can full of dough, landing on the back of my head.

"That was impressive," Sissy said, peering over Cindy's shoulder and past my feet, which were resting on the lip of the can. "What're *you* doing here?" she asked Cindy.

"You Peppers sure are a suspicious bunch," Cindy said. She turned on her heel and strode away. I craned my neck, peering around the dough can, watching her ass jiggle under tight polyester.

"She's a lesbian, you moron," Sissy said, hands on hips.

"I'm a bi-SEX-yoo-ul!" Cindy sang from out front, letting loose a torrent of giggles.

"Look at you. You're pathetic," Sissy said. She walked around the dough can and gave me a hand up. "I should leave you on the floor next time. Maybe you'd learn something."

"I doubt it," I said, rubbing the back of my head.

"I do, too," Sissy said. "Turn around." I turned around. She felt the bump. "I'll get some ice." She went back up front. I jerked the dough can up onto its wheels, then rolled it up front and shoved it in its place under the dough flattener. Sissy came round the corner with a plastic baggie of ice. I took it from her.

"God, you can be such a dumb jerk sometimes," she said.

I adjusted the ice bag on the back on my head. The industrial air conditioner blew as hard as it could, but it was still a feverish 85 degrees inside. The ice bag felt good.

Sissy stared knives and hand grenades at me. "Stay away from her," she said. "There's your nickel's worth of free advice for the day." Sissy was right. But that didn't mean anything to a seventeen-year-old kid jazzed on hormones.

Cindy sat down on the other end of the make table, where we made the Cavatini pasta and meatball sandwiches, swinging her feet playfully. "I dig watching you work," she said. "The way you twitch around. You're such a strange little dude. And when you talk—shit! You say the strangest things."

"Stay away from my brother!" Sissy said, pulling a pizza out of the oven to cut up and take out to the dining area. She waved a pair of pliers in the air.

"Or what?"

"Just stay away from him. You got it?" She hoisted the pizza, bubbling and steaming, over to the cutting board, then slid it out of the tin onto the board. The boiling sauce and cheese sloshed over the side. She scraped the pizza lava back onto the crust with the pizza cutter.

"You may have everyone else in here intimidated, but not me," Cindy said. "What's some 15-year-old hotshot gonna do to me?" Cindy was still relaxed, swinging her feet.

Sissy quickly sheared the pizza into eight slices. "You'll find out if you don't stay away from my brother," she said, plopping the steaming mess onto a serving tray. Then she growled and stomped away. She didn't like being put in the position of having to defend me.

"Cindy," I said, my palms up toward her. "Listen ... " I couldn't think of anything beyond that to say. Maybe I wanted to tell her not to pay attention to Sissy. Or maybe

I wanted to tell her that Sissy had a point.

"No, no," she interrupted. "I *like* a challenge." She hopped down from the make table. "C'mere." She curled an index finger at me.

"No," I said.

"I'm not gonna bite you," she said. "C'mere."

I shook my head and glanced over at the ice baggie, which I'd dropped on the make table. It was just a blob of water now, like I'd won a goldfish at the fair, but the goldfish had gone on the lam.

"Just for a second," she said, squaring her shoulders. "You're such a sweet little boy. I'm under indictment for corrupting Sarasota's youth, you know." She showed me a mock angry face, lowering her chin. "Don't make me come over there."

I swallowed. For once, I had nothing smart to say. I thought that if I could just reach into my wallet and pop that last tiny Valium that I had stashed in there, I would be all right. But I couldn't reach into my back pocket for wallet—no, too obvious. Besides, I was shaking so much I'd probably drop it. "Be nice," I said shyly, my voice shaking apart. "Be nice to me."

"Oh, honey," she said, "that is just so cute." She came over, took my hands and pulled me into the back. Before I could, I don't know, she was kissing me sweetly, then less sweetly. It was almost an out of body experience, floating.

She suddenly pulled back. "You still have that van?" she asked.

"Van?" I asked.

"Van," she said. "Give me a ride home?"

I could smell pizzas burning.

All of a sudden Chuck's voice said, "Welcome back, Cindy." He'd snuck back and was playing with a register tape. "Looks like you're back to your old tricks."

"Chuckmeister, how are you?" Cindy said, giving me the tiniest push away. She reached into her front pocket and handed him a sandwich bag. "As promised," she purred.

"These pizzas are burning!" Sissy shrieked from up front.

I ran and pulled them out of the oven. They were a little burned, but not too bad. Thin and extra-crispy?

Our shift was over and we were relieved by Albino and Wayner. Wayner was our only waiter. He was a heavy-metal guy with the hair and tattoos, and muttonchops braided down past his chin. Sort of prissy, though. Sissy told me he was a fruit because he never hit on her.

"That doesn't sound fair," I told her.

"It's not fair, but it is the test," Sissy said. We went out back to smoke.

"But he must be over 30," I said.

"So?"

"Chuck's over 30 and he's never hit on you," I said.

She rolled her eyes at that one.

"You're telling me ... "

She shook her head yes. "But I turned him down. It's all copasetic," she said.

"Who else has, you know?" I asked.

"Teachers. Dirty old men. Bums sleeping at the public library," Sissy said, ticking them off on her fingers. "I don't know. *Non-gay men*." She gave me one of those looks. "What're you gonna do? Kick every man's ass so you can protect my honor?"

I shrugged.

"That's your answer to everything," she said.

"It seems to be the only one I can think up," I said. We pushed outside through the back door. The aroma of yeast and garlic filled the air, along with the smell of ink from the print shop next door. Cars burbled past on Bee Ridge Road. Across the road was a Winn Dixie, which anchored a cheap strip mall. The Winn Dixie was always filled with sparrows and robins that'd hopped in through the automated doors, and flew in great swirls over the stacks of merchandise. They would light upon cereal boxes and pyramids of canned corn, watching you shop, and then would flit away when you got too close. Sissy sucked on one of her Merits.

"I'm giving Cindy a lift home," I told her.

"Sometimes you make it hard to love you, Buzz," she

said, exhaling a cloud of smoke. She was the only person I knew who talked about love.

The back door swung open. Cindy peered round the corner at us, her hand on the knob. "I'm ready to jet when you are," she said.

Sissy flicked the remains of the cigarette at the print shop. It tumbled end over and sparked on the gravel. Presses chugged and cranked. "Just remember," she said to neither of us, or both of us, tilting her head back and watching a plane high above excrete a vapor trail, "I warned you."

After a tense drive, we dropped Sissy off at home. She climbed down from the passenger seat of the van and gave me another tired warning look. I sent back the puzzled shrug. The door slammed. Cindy climbed into the now vacant front seat.

"What's with her?" Cindy asked. She tossed her feet on the dash and dug a joint and a lighter out of her purse. The joint had been hidden in a Sucrets tin.

"She's okay," I said, driving hurriedly away from the house. I didn't want my mother to see me like this.

"She treats you like a pet dog," Cindy said.

"No she doesn't," I snapped.

"Okay, cool out. No need to go all defensive on me," Cindy said. "So you know where the Circusland Trailer Park is, right?" She passed me the joint. I took a few tentative puffs, leaning down below the dash for a moment. I resurfaced and handed back the joint. It went out.

"North on Beneva. Across the street from the all-you-can-eat Swedish joint," I said.

"Right," Cindy said, sparking it back up.

I felt, unexpectedly, clearheaded and strong. "That's some primo stuff."

"Yeah, well, don't get used to it," Cindy said. She took a couple more tokes then put it out on the tip of her tongue. "The guy we're going to see? I've been crashing at his place, but I've got a new place now and I just need a little help moving a couple of things."

"Moving?"

"Just a lamp, a futon mattress. Maybe a chair or two," Cindy said. "He's, sort of, my source."

"I'm helping you move out from a drug dealer?" I yelped.

"Listen, it's no big deal. Wait 'til you meet this guy," she said, laughing. She adjusted the side view mirror and applied some blood red lipstick, smacked her lips. "Don't look so panicky," she said. "Shit. You want me to torch that roach back up for you?" She had her purse open, like she was ready to dig it out again.

"No," I said. *On the other hand*, I thought, *maybe it would be better to be lit up when this guy broke my face.*

She snapped the purse shut and dropped it onto

the dash. Then she slid out of her seat and came over to me. I made a left-hand turn and almost got hit by an oncoming car, which blasted its horn at me. Cindy was unfazed, steadying herself on the center console as she slid her fingers through my hair with one hand and lightly grasped my chin with the other. She kissed my cheek, my forehead. We pulled up to a light. She kissed my mouth, my chin.

"Courage, little man," she whispered.

The Circusland Trailer Park was a mess of colorful, beaten trailers surrounded by trampolines, and circus clothes hung out to dry on lines strung between Australian pines. We parked next to the seediest trailer, dented white aluminum somewhere underneath all the soot.

"Albert Junior!" Cindy shrieked when the door opened up. Albert Junior was built like a major household appliance, short and stocky, but solid. A filthy beard rimmed his chin. A wispy birdshit mustache dripped off his upper lip. Neat pockmarks were drilled into his reddish forehead and cheeks. Blond hair cascaded off his skull. He was, for the most part, deathly white, wearing a Hawaiian shirt, cargo shorts and Birkenstocks, none of which had been cleaned since he'd bought them, by the looks of it.

"So, you're leaving me for *him*?" he whined.

"Of course not," Cindy said. She flipped her hair over

her shoulder and followed Albert Junior inside.

"But he's a kid," Albert Junior said. "Look at him." I was standing in the doorway of the trailer, a foot dangling behind me, steadying myself with both hands on the jamb, unsure whether to stay or to bolt. Looking inside, I'd never seen so many bongs in my life, not even at Subterranean Circus, the head shop just north of the county line. "He must be wearing half a tube of your lipstick on his face."

"So fucking what? Grab that chair over there, Buzz," Cindy said. She poked me, and nodded in the direction of the chair. It was covered with faded upholstery, a sheet of clear plastic stapled on top, the wooden legs chipped and scraped. I picked it up and headed for the door.

"You're leaving me for a kid named Buzz. I can't believe I fucking bailed you out."

"Believe it, Junior, you sissy-shit asshole."

"That's my chair," Albert Junior said, planting himself in front of the doorway.

"Dude, I don't want to fight you," I said.

"Don't call me 'dude,' you-you-you," and his brain gave out. He took a deep breath and looked around, then seemed to forget why he was standing in the doorway. He stepped out of the way and I walked through with the chair aimed at him, like a lion tamer.

"That's classic," Cindy said.

I tossed the chair in the back of the van, then studied my face in the side view mirror. "Oh, shit," I said. I found a paper napkin on the floor of the van and wiped my face off as best I could. I went back inside.

Cindy shoved something in the front pocket of my pants. It gave me a jolt to have her hand that close to my dick, even if it was just for a second. "Shhh," she went. We slipped back to the bedroom and rolled up a thin futon mattress that was spread across the cigarette-burned carpet, and tied it with a laundry cord that hung across the tiny room. Filled ashtrays and cut-up Coke cans littered the floor. There were a few dresses in the closet. A window unit hummed, dripping out a dull stream of coolish air. A hotel painting hung crooked on the wall. In it, a Tom Sawyerish boy lolled next to a stream, chewing on a piece of grass, staring at his own reflection. A mill churned water nearby. A cocker spaniel puppy frolicked across flower-strewn turf. It was bullshit nostalgia for an America that never was. Cindy caught me glaring at it. "It came with the trailer," she said. "Sometimes I wonder what he's thinking about."

"Smallpox," I said. "Typhoid. Fucking a goat. Killing Indians. Setting that dog's tail on fire. Lynching a black man."

"Where the hell did that come from?" Cindy said, shocked. It was my turn to knock her off her heels.

"I hate nostalgia. My dad gets totally choked up

about the '50's. He must miss polio, fallout shelter drills, communist witch hunts and shitty, Pat Boone-bastardized pop tunes."

"You're a weird, little guy," she said, face aglitter. "Let me freshen up those lipstick marks." And she kissed me roughly, pushing me against the wall, my head knocking into the faux-innocent boy from faux-innocent times. She lifted a leg and kneed the wall, grinding her hips into mine. She was my height, but probably outweighed me by fifteen pounds. The kiss was better than the super-pot she'd shared with me in the van. She pulled back and said, "Grab the other end of this and let's go." She tossed the dresses on top. We passed by Albert Junior, who'd fallen asleep in a Kmart lounge chair.

My whole body, my soul, was whirring voltage.

After we lugged the bedding to the car, she went running back in for a moment and emerged holding a bong by the neck.

"Let's go," she shouted, then started laughing musically. "He'll never miss it, the prick." I backed the van out, jammed it in first, and floored it, spinning up trailer park dust.

Dick for Brains

"There's something wrong with me," I said, my back to her. The futon mattress sagged toward the middle; we'd have to fluff it up at some point. "Whatever it is, I don't think I can fix it." The room was partitioned off with a translucent bed sheet that clung to two nails in the wall.

She said, "I know."

The 8-track clunked along to Pink Floyd. *And after all, we're only ordinary men.* Everyone I knew had that goddamned album.

"I ought to give you a haircut. It's a tangled bush."

"Don't bother," I said.

"I'd like to," she said.

We were nude under a sticky sheet. My ribs stuck out pathetically. The rest of my body was nearly hairless, smooth and white. I was deathly pale for a Floridian. A palmetto bug scuttled across the linoleum in the kitchen. A fan churned stale air. Cindy fingertipped the edge of my ear. I could feel a sweat-drip run down the back of my neck.

How did we get this far? I never wanted someone as much as I wanted her, yet, when we were, you know, doing it, a black sadness had crept into me and shut me down. On top of that, she had just told me she would have to go back to New Hampshire to take care of her father, who just found out he had pancreatic cancer. "I don't know when I'll be back," she said.

"You won't be back," I said, bitterly. My family had moved around a lot when I was a little kid. I'd taught myself not to get too attached to places and people.

"I'm sorry," she said.

I rolled over to face her. "Don't be sorry. Now I can brag about this to all my high school pals. How I scored," I said.

"But you won't," she said.

"What makes you so sure," I said, trying to look cocky.

"Because you have the lowest tolerance for bullshit of anyone I ever met," she said. "Especially when you're the bullshit artist."

"Everyone has me pegged," I said, rolling onto my back and slipping my hands behind my head. The ceiling had a brown, Australia-shaped stain embedded in it.

She got up and padded to the bathroom. Ghostly light shined through the frosted window and filtered through the pale blue shower curtain. I could see her legs, and could hear her peeing. The intimacy of it was appalling and wonderful.

She shouted something.

"What?" I shouted back.

She wiped herself. The toilet flushed. She padded back toward me. "The original angry young man," she said, getting back into bed with me and tossing the sheet over us. "I'll tell you a secret. I knew I couldn't get married in Massachusetts. I only wanted to lure her away for a while."

"Really?"

"Yeah, really," she said. She drew a circle on my chest with her index finger. "Now it's your turn. You tell me a secret." She licked and bit a nipple.

"Um," I went. I tried to think of one. My body vibrated.

"There's your problem," she said, tossing the sheet off, then straddling me on her knees as I palmed her thighs. She reached between our legs. "Let's make the false start our secret," she said, beginning to grind. "This time's the real first time."

Afterwards, she dug the package out of my pants' pocket. It looked like rabbit turds. It was hash. We smoked it out of the bong she'd stolen from Albert Junior, lighting and relighting and lighting, sitting cross-legged on the peeling, yellow linoleum. Then we took a shower together, feeling mellow and tender. "You weren't a bad lay for a first-timer," she told me as we toweled off.

"But you've had better," I said.

"Sorry, kid," she said.

She tossed a halter dress over her head, snapped on some panties, and slipped on a pair of sandals. I put my stinking Pizza Hut clothes back on, leaving the smock unzipped. We sat down in the kitchen.

Her roommate came in the door carrying a paper sack of groceries, jangling keys. She didn't seem surprised to see me. She had a severe crew cut, dyed black. Reddish razor stubble spouted all over her bare legs. She wore a black pocket tee shirt tucked into khaki cut-offs.

"Hi, Buzz," she said. Cindy and I were both still damp from the shower.

"Yeah?" I went.

"I'm Darlene," she said. She had a soft, feminine face and a musical voice.

"Hey, Darlene," I said.

She set the groceries down on the counter. "So you get Cindy all settled in?" She and Cindy exchanged a look.

"Yeah," I said. "Except for her chair. She made me leave it out in the van."

"So Cindy," Darlene asked in a mocking tone, sitting down with us at the circular kitchen table, "when's your court date?"

"Never," Cindy said. "You need some help with those groceries?"

"What do you mean 'never'?" I asked.

"Albert Junior's attorney assured Bunni's parents that we'd make the trial a public spectacle. So they arranged a plea bargain. I got time served. There's a restraining order, too. Probation," Cindy said. "You want me to put those groceries away?" She leaned back in her chair.

"You don't know where anything goes," Darlene said. She turned to me. "Can you *believe* her?"

"Not for a second," I said.

"You're right," Darlene said to Cindy. "He *is* a snotty little fuck."

"He's kinda cute, though, isn't he?" Cindy said.

"He has girl eyes," Darlene commented, studying me. She got up and put the groceries away. The ice cream was already starting to melt. "Anyone want some herbal tea?" She filled up the kettle and set it on the stovetop, clicked on the burner.

"You have any real tea?" I asked. "I don't like drinking that hippie swill."

"Listen to this guy," Darlene said, smiling and chuckling it up. "'Hippie swill.'" She mussed my hair a bit. It was almost dry. "Yeah, we have some Lipton for you, Mister Man."

After the whistle blew, she poured three mugs. We dunked our teabags and blew into the mugs. I sat staring at Cindy, who returned my stare with a rueful look.

"Perfection is oppression," Darlene said.

"What?" I said, snapping out of the trance.

"I mean, look at her. Like you have been," Darlene said. "She's too perfect. I could never really care for someone that perfect looking." Darlene finished off her mug and put it in the sink.

"Anyone for a swim?"

Cindy was a little pissed now. "Swim?"

"Where?" I asked.

"North Lido," Darlene said. "Where else?" North Lido was the topless beach on Longboat Key. It had been legendary when I was in junior high. After a Sarasota boy obtained his learner's permit, he would make the pilgrimage to North Lido looking for hot topless chicks. He was sorely disappointed, as all he found were saggy, elderly Euros in Speedos, ugly dykes, and middle-aged fruits.

"I don't have a suit with me," I said.

"We'll stop by Zayre's on the way," Darlene said. "Come on. Cindy's going. Aren't you Cindy?"

"Perfect," Cindy spat. Her arms and legs were crossed, her face dark. Her foot bounced quickly.

"I was only saying," Darlene said. She beamed, happy to have scratched something in Cindy. "C'mon," Darlene said, walking up behind me and placing her hand on my head. "Don't you want to take your new pet for a walk?"

The darkness passed from Cindy's face, replaced by resignation. "Sure," Cindy said. "What the hell."

"Pet," I said.

"Don't be a bummer," Darlene said, scratching my scalp gently.

I shrugged. Resignation was a way of life for me, for all of us.

If you can imagine a store even shittier and more low rent than Kmart, then you can imagine Zayre's. The pavement around the store and in the parking lot was cracked and busted, and all the yellow lines that once denoted parking spots were faded and chipped away. Three of the other stores sharing the strip mall were closed, butcher paper taped inside their windows.

Once inside, under slowly turning ceiling fans, buzzing florescent lighting and weak industrial cooling, the women decided to play dress-up with me. They picked out a short-sleeved purple velour pullover, fake Jordache jeans, a pair of earth shoes and rainbow socks, and made me put it all on. It was humiliating. Eventually, a pair of swim trunks were held up to my midsection and we went to the front to pay.

The clerk, not much older than me, was leaning on the conveyer belt reading the *Weekly World News* while spinning a piece of gum from her mouth around her index finger. She glanced up and snorted back a laugh. Darlene pushed me from behind. I had more tags hanging off me than Minnie Pearl.

"What he has on and this swimsuit," Cindy said, slapping a credit card on the counter.

The clerk slipped the tabloid under the counter and rang us up. I had to proffer my bottom so she could see the jeans' price, and pull off one of the shoes and hand it to her for the same reason. She checked the credit card against a mimeographed list of numbers in a three-ring binder next to the register, then snapped the credit card and receipt into the holder and shoved across the handle. Cindy signed, and the clerk handed us an empty bag with a stapled-on receipt.

We ambled outside into the blasting sunshine as I prayed that no one I knew would see me dressed this way. At least we'd be at the beach soon and I could put on the cheap trunks and shove these alien clothes inside the van.

Cindy yanked the tags off me and dropped them on the ground. "Let's boogie," she said. She really was perfect. Just looking at her got me higher than anything I'd ever popped, drank or inhaled.

The two women strolled in front of me toward the van. The sun angled across their bodies, through the sundresses, revealing their figures. I was overwhelmed. Then, for an instant, I nearly came to my senses. I didn't trust this feeling. It was too much like joy. I thought, *Holy shit what the hell am I doing? Run, boy! Run!* My high was evaporating in the heat. Then Darlene spun around and waved at me, shouting, "C'mon! We're running out of daylight!" I slipped back into my trance. "Dick for brains, dick for brains, why'm I your dick for brains," I sang on my way to the van.

We rolled down Bee Ridge, down to US 41 and took it north, past Sarasota High, past the park and the marina, then took a left at the Admiral Benbow Inn. We crossed the bridge and drove around St. Armand's Circle. I parked in the Lido Beach public parking area.

Darlene and Cindy quickly unassed the van and dragged out all our supplies—a Styrofoam cooler filled with beer, some towels and a green army blanket. Even from the northernmost parking area, the beach was a bit of a walk. The sun was getting ready to dunk into the gulf. The sky was streaked orange and purple.

"I gotta change," I said. "Where'm I supposed to change?"

"In the trees?" Darlene offered.

"In the van," Cindy said. "Just lie down. No one will see you. We'll stand guard."

I closed the sliding door, dropped to my back and stripped out of my clothes. As I pulled up my trunks, leaning on my head and arching my back, I noticed Darlene looking in at me through the back window. I felt a flicker of embarrassment. *How old is she?* I wondered.

I hopped out of the van then leapt right back in. The pavement was hot enough to cook your feet. I slipped the earth shoes back on.

Cindy and Darlene were already halfway to the woods that separated Lido Beach from North Lido. They carried the cooler with the towels and blanket heaped on top between them. I ran to catch up. "Can I carry anything?" I asked.

"You honestly don't remember me, do you?" Darlene asked.

"Remember you? Did you used to work at the Hut?" I asked.

"No. I graduated last year. From the Catholic high school?" She stared straight ahead as we entered the woods. Brown pine needles crunched underfoot.

"I guess I don't," I said.

"I saw you at Sarasota Square Mall. With your sister? I waved to you and you didn't wave back? I work at the Thom McAnn's?"

"Sorry," I said. I hated that mall.

"Yeah, well," Darlene said. And we walked the rest of the way in silence. Small towns. Things like that happen in them.

We reached the white sand. North Lido hadn't changed. Same people as always, except for us. Cindy and Darlene set down the cooler and spread out the blanket. I slipped off the faggot shoes. We each grabbed a beer. The women pulled the dresses off over their heads. Darlene made a dash for the water. Cindy and I sat down with our beers.

"So, um," I went. "Uh, how did you two meet?"

"You think there's something between me and Darlene?"

"Well, yeah." My face felt prickly.

"Why? Because she's letting me crash at her place for a week or two?"

"Sure," I said.

"There could never be anything between me and Darlene," Cindy said. "For one thing, she's a breeder, through and through. For another, no one's ever hurt her."

"No one's ever hurt me," I said.

"Someone's hurt you," she said. "You wear it like a badge." We watched Darlene frolic in the water. "Baggage. All these girls I went to college with used to talk about how they didn't want a guy with baggage. Well, I don't give a fuck for people who don't have baggage."

"What about Bunni?"

"Bunni needed me," Cindy said. She grimaced. "Her daddy's been fucking her the past two years."

"Jesus," I went. I changed the subject: "You went to college?"

"Don't look so shocked. University of New Hampshire, Class of '79."

"Weird," I said.

"It's not so weird. I majored in philosophy. You should,

too. It gets your brain limber. Better than all that shit you smoke," she said.

"So how did you meet Darlene?"

"How do I meet anybody? She used to buy pot from me," Cindy said. She reclined onto the blanket and closed her eyes. "Lay down next to me," she said.

Darlene finished her beer and tossed the empty toward the woods. She came running back for another one. I opened the cooler and tossed a cold one up to her. "Thanks," she said, popping it open. "You really don't remember me?"

"Sure," I said. "I remember you."

"Don't lie," she said. "You're not good at it."

Cindy snickered. Sweat beads popped out all over her.

Darlene sat down next to me. Her feet were wet and coated with sand. "You always ate lunch alone, sitting under that tree by the gym."

"I'm sorry I don't remember you," I said. Then I did remember her. She had had long red hair. She was one of the only girls to wear a miniskirt to school, and had a too-even sunlamp tan. "We were in Spanish class together," I said.

"That's right," she said, getting excited. "I knew you'd remember me."

"You don't have the tan anymore, or the hair," I said.

"Yeah," she said, running her fingers over her razor cut. "C'mon. Let's go in." She got up and extended a hand toward me.

"No, thanks," I said. The truth was I hated the beach. I didn't like the seagulls constantly attacking me, or the sand up my ass, or getting a blistery sunburn that took a week to heal. I didn't like the people there, or the music they played. The last time I had been at the beach was at that Greek/Italian party, when I had gotten annihilated on Ouzo and tried to drown myself. Dave had to swim out to a sandbar and drag me back in. How long ago was that? It seemed like forever.

"Suit yourself," she said, and ran out into the gulf, galloping through the waves.

Night came quickly. All our beer was gone. I staggered around and wandered into the trees. I collected branches, twigs, needles, and dumped them in front of our blanket. I went back to the woods and found more. I scooped out a little trench around the mess of flammable stuff and set it on fire with Cindy's lighter. A couple came over. They had Boone's Farm Country Quencher. We passed the bottle around. Blue sparks, red flames. Bugs stayed away from us. Somebody brought over more wood. More people sat down. We pulled the blanket back as the fire took on more life. I got up, went into the woods and took a leak. I walked back to the van and got the old chair out. I staggered back through the woods, tripping around, and navigated my way out, aiming myself at the fire.

"What are you doing?" Cindy asked me.

I heaved the old chair into the fire. A flurry of red sparks clouded the air. The chair was devoured.

"I was going to give you that chair!" Cindy shouted. "It was my mother's! It was the only thing I had left of her! Why did you do that?"

"I don't know," I said, confused. I balled my hands in front of my chest, contrite.

"You don't know?" Cindy went. The air pissed out of her. She slumped down on the blanket. Maybe a dozen people were gathered around the fire now. They were all silent. They didn't want Cindy to be a bummer. "Ah, what the hell," she said at last. People started talking again. The air buzzed.

The AM radio tinkled out the hits. My baby takes the morning train. I love a rainy night. I pulled into the driveway. I took off the earth shoes and tossed them in the road. I walked inside wearing only a pair of sandy swim trunks.

My mother was waiting up for me. "Where have you been?" she snapped, careful to keep her voice low. If she woke my father, there'd be hell to pay for both of us.

"Out," I said. I tried to brush past her. She was stronger than that. She stepped in front of me.

"You're drunk," she said.

"Of course not," I said. "I was at the beach with

some friends."

"Some floozy. Some lesbian floozy who ran off with a little girl," my mother said. Sissy had ratted me out. Probably had shown her the newspaper clipping. I could just imagine it.

"Where's your brother?"

"Helping some girl from work move."

"What girl?"

"She's not really a girl. She's a waitress."

"A waitress?"

"You remember that girl who ran off with another girl to get married? Teenage lesbian manhunt? It was in the paper." The paper is offered up.

"Let me see that."

"I need to take a shower," I said.

"You're not seeing that … that *old lady* again," my mother said.

"She's only twenty-six," I said. "That's not much older than I am, really." There it was. My tactical error. I confessed so much in that one little sentence. I was an idiot.

"Twenty-six!" my mother exploded. "Twenty-six? She's a pervert! What does she want with little boys?"

"The age difference is less than ten years," I said. "I'm not so little."

"Ten years, ten thousand years!" Mom roared. "It doesn't make a difference! She's some kind of weirdo!"

"What the hell is going on out there?" my father hollered. It froze us for a moment. We were both so well trained. We shared a conspiratorial look.

"Nothing," my mother yelled back contritely. "Go back to sleep." We both waited. When we felt the silence settle back, she hissed, "You will *never* see that *woman* again. Do you understand? If you have to quit that job, you'll quit that job. But you will *never see her again*. Never. Do you understand me?"

"Yes," I said. She didn't have to tell me what would happen if I saw Cindy again. My father would get involved. No one in this world wanted that.

She was staring a hole right through me, my mother.

Deny Everything

Our parents took off to Ohio without us. Another one of our relatives was dying, or some bullshit like that. Sparky came home from college for the summer and, being Joe Responsible, was put in charge for the week and a half our parents were gone. Which was too fucking bad for him.

"Events have been set in motion," Sissy said, poking him in the chest. "Kegs have been procured. Pizzas stolen. People invited."

"I can still spank you," Sparky said.

"Grow up, Mr. Spock," Sissy said. "Why don't you say something?" Sissy asked me.

"What'm I supposed to say?" I asked. "Get him, tiger?" I was sprawled out on the ratty sofa, watching *I Dream of Jeannie*. "I don't get why this guy isn't totally grooving on having this hot magical chick living in his house," I said. "Why isn't he ordering up gold bricks, booze, dope, mansions and swimming pools? All his whining gets on my nerves."

"Why did I ask for his help?" Sissy asked Sparky.

"Beats me," Sparky said.

"A helicopter," I said. "I could get off on having a helicopter."

They went into the kitchen to continue their argument, which Sissy would win because she won every goddamned argument.

Major Nelson yowled, "Jeannie!" "Dumbass," I commented, grabbing a handful of Cheetos.

The party commenced after dark. Sissy and I were cooking the pizzas while Albino dragged the kegs out of my van and set them up in washtubs full of ice. He bought a case of Miller in glass bottles for the consumption of the chosen few—everyone else would drink out of wax paper to-go cups, courtesy of Pizza Hut.

I went out back and helped Albino attach the little pumps to the kegs, then helped him sample some brew. We got pretty wasted, actually, and dug through my piles of 45s. We'd bought most of them from this guy up in Bradenton who ran a head shop/record store. We'd bopped in there one day to buy lousy rock music, dissatisfied with the lousy rock music we already owned. The fat hippie prick behind the counter said, "over there," as soon as we walked in the door. We had no idea what he was talking about, but did as ordered. We went *over there*, to a pile of records that changed our lives.

"Look at this," Albino said to me. "This one's called,

'Blitzkrieg Bop.'"

"This one's called, 'The Dicks Hate the Police,'" I said, holding it up.

The covers were of people screaming in pain, or 1950's suburbanites set on fire, or cops arresting teenagers. If there was a band photo, they looked just like us. I'm not talking about the clothes or haircuts. Style is a corporate trap, motherfucker, another way for the rich to extort money out of you. I'm talking about the looks on their faces.

We tore ass home and slapped the offensive material on our turntables. These bands were trapped in this shitty world. Their dads were fucking alcoholics, their moms doped up by pharmaceutical companies. Corporations gunned for them. Toxic fumes in suburbia. Cops with nightsticks. Killer rednecks. They were looking forward to getting nuked. They sounded like us.

They *were* us.

We didn't know what to call our little group or ourselves. Ten, fifteen years later we would be labeled "alternative" by jokers our age who just didn't get it, and by the ex-hippies who mass-marketed the outer gloss of our lives for the global mega-merger corporations.

But we did know what to call the people who crashed the scene and who didn't belong there. A few of them had already shown up at our party, hair dyed blue or some shit, razorblades dangling, dressed in expensive outfits exhibiting a sense of style borrowed from the English. Fucking *trendoids*.

"The worst thing about trendoids is their condescension," Albino said. We were in the garage now, hiding, and had taken the bottled beer with us. "Most trendoids are nerds or other social incompetents who desperately want to be one of the popular, beautiful people. They wish they could be Biff or Buffy, but they're not. So they descend to our level, like we're gonna be grateful. Like they're gonna be the king or queen of the ball with us 'cause we're such obvious losers." Albino was grinding his teeth now, getting himself worked up. "But they don't understand one fucking thing about us. Because the thing we hate the most is popularity."

"Anarchy now," I said and swigged my beer. The cigarette in my other hand burned down to my fingers. I flicked the butt at the lawn mower, hoping for the worst. It died in midair.

"Fucking A-right, anarchy now," Albino growled. "King, queen, prince, princess. Jackie O! Celebrity worship! Fuck that! I want to burn all that shit down. And those little fascists who dress like 'punks,' who are The Man Who Would Be King, they're even worse than those popular fuckers who want your sister."

"Bite your tongue," I said, egging him on.

"Motherfucker, those chess club rejects would kill you, stick you in a gas fucking chamber if one of those Biffs or Buffys told them that everyone was fucking doing it. That's how the Nazis took over in Germany, man! Coolness killed my people over there. Or rather, uncool fuckers who wanted desperately to be cool!" Albino was totally shaking with rage. His mom was a Warsaw ghetto escapee. One of her tamest stories was about standing next to a river at the end of the war, poking the bodies that were floating past with a stick. She told that one to us while cutting the crust off a PB&J she'd just prepared for Albino. He chugged the rest of his beer and savagely smashed the bottle against the wall. This is why I liked him so much. He made me seem levelheaded sometimes.

"Dude," I said, "chill out. This is supposed to be a party."

"Let's kick a trendoid's ass," Albino demanded.

"If you're feeling aggressive," I said, handing him a hammer, "beat on Buster's (as I liked to call my father in mixed company) air compressor." I nodded toward it. "I've been working on the valve up top there."

"You have some big fucking problems with your old man," Albino commented. "Man."

"You know where he got the money for it," I said.

"If you tell that story one more time, I'm gonna hit you with this hammer," Albino said. Then he walked over and beat on the valve a few times.

Since you're dying to know:

Once upon a time, ol' Buzz was low on green. So he took his passbook down to his friendly neighborhood Sarasota Savings and Loan and asked for twenty bucks. The pants-suited lady behind the counter said, "But you cannot have the twenty bucks."

"Forsooth," goes our hero, "Why for can't I have my moolah? It says right here that I have $958 in my account. It is typed plain as day."

"But you are a minor," sayeth the bitch. "And your father is co-signer! And you have naught but five smackeroonis!"

Alas, our Buzz goes home to confront his fat, pig, alcoholic, fuckhead, can't-hold-a-goddamned-job father, who is playing with a brand-new air compressor, driving nails into a sheet of plywood with a brand-new pneumatic nail gun.

"Where's my money?" Buzz whines, already knowing the answer.

Buster, the aforementioned fat, pig, alcoholic, fuckhead, can't-hold-a-goddamned-job father, says, "Too bad. This ain't a free ride, kid." And snickers.

And there's nothing much Buzz could do about it except to try and sabotage every aspect of his father's life. Starting off with beating on the compressor in spots that are not obvious to drunken idiot daddies. And continuing on to microwaving Cheez Whiz,

Buster's favorite treat, into cement cheez pudding; pouring sugar in the gas tank of Buster's 1979 Pontiac Grand Am, and poking tiny holes in the radiator, and tapping sand into the automatic steering fluid, and pulling loose the threads from the dove-gray leatherette seating; loosening the tiny screws of dad-dad-daddy-o's prescription glasses so that the lenses constantly fall out; nicely shaking up his shitty Red, White and Blue beer; hiding in the bushes across the street and shooting him in his fat ass with Sparky's BB gun one night, and watching him reach around to scratch at the wound; using his gift of mimicry to pretend to be a prostitute (paid for by Buster) offering her services to a number of customers in Buster's address book, most not appreciating the perk Buster was providing, and not showing up at the Normandy motel after making a date with the one who did; jamming a roll of pennies in Buster's shotgun and cocking it; placing tiny garlic bulbs in the pockets of his polyester suits and cooking them in with a hot iron; subtly bending his golf clubs with vice grips; and, of course, just plain old spitting in his food every chance he got.

And Buzz lived crappily ever after. The end.

"You don't seem to have any problems with your old man," I noted.

"He sells cigarettes out of vending machines in bars,"

Albino said. "What possible problems could I have with a man like that?"

"There's always gonna be spare change around," I said.

"And cigarettes. You want a quarter?" Albino asked. He flipped one over.

I caught it and pocketed it.

"Give it back, motherfucker," Albino went. "And no comments about 'cheap Jews' either."

I handed it back to him.

We were out of beer, and had to brave the party, our own fucking party, and the fucking trendoids, to get more. A couple of mostly devoured, and cooked and reheated and burnt Pizza Hut pizzas graced the kitchen counter. I remembered what our manager Chuck once told me about cheap pizza, "You serve dog shit pizza, and as long as it's half-price, these bastards will eat it." It was Half-Price Family Night when he said that, and every redneck family in town was there, having a plain cheese pizza, along with a pitcher of water for the wife and kids, and an eight-ounce draft for hardworking pa. The waitresses called it No-Tip Inbred Night.

The beautiful people were out in the back yard, listening to Journey or REO Speedwagon or Boston or Foreigner on my parents' hi-fi, conveniently set-up outside where it would annoy the neighbors long into the night. The jocks whooped and hollered "yeah," because if they didn't, they wouldn't be having a totally awesome time. "Par-TAY! Yeah!" Soon enough, they would strip off their shirts to show off their fine, fine musculature. The preps might get adventurous and take a few tentative puffs off someone else's marijuana cigarette. Oh, my! A wonderful time had by all. Would I become, um, popular now? If only!

All my vinyl was out there too, and I thought. "Shit, my records!" It was too much to bear, thinking of those cocksuckers pawing through my stuff. But then I heard *Guilty! Guilty!* playing. I poked my head around the corner and saw Dave sitting on the nice couch in the museum room, where no one was allowed to tread. "Dave!" I shouted.

"Hey, man," Dave said, his eyes glazed nicely. It was the first time I'd seen him since his Jesus-Don't-Like-Drugs treatment. The couple of times we'd tried to see him since he got back, his mother had chased us off, once, most memorably, wielding a baseball bat, joint hanging out of her mouth, eyes crazy with amphetamines, as she shrieked inhumanly at us. "You did it to my son! You did it!" We couldn't help but laugh as we jogged and stumbled toward the van.

"I guess the Lord's word didn't take," I said.

He shrugged. "Yeah, fuck it."

"Where you working?" I asked as Albino handed me a beer.

"I'm working at this Christian restaurant, baking pies," Dave said. "Got my GED, moved out. Living with this dude in a trailer. It's copasetic."

I took a stab. "Albert Junior?"

"How'd you know?"

"Lucky guess," I said.

"Guess who's a waitress there," Dave went, passing me the joint he was working on.

It was good shit. "Dunno."

"Bunni," Albino said. I handed him the joint. He thumbed toward the corner. Sure enough, there she was, slumped over, nodding in and out. Her face was caked with makeup, and crumbling cracks appeared in her smile lines and around her eyes and her forehead. Albino handed down the doob. The room sparkled.

"Yeah, Bunni," Dave said. "She's totally into chicks now. Went to the same rehab place I did. Fucking weirdass prison." Dave gaped up at us, zonked. "What was I talking about?"

Albino smacked me on the arm. "Let's go see her."

I followed him over and we crouched down. Bunni was wicked wasted. I reached over and pinched her cheek. "Hey, Bunni-Wunnie," I went.

Her eyes cracked open. "Heyyyyy, Buzz," she went in super slo-mo. "Hi-yee."

"I hear they're selling marriage licenses for faggots in Alaska," Albino said. "It should only take you a few days to get there by rowboat."

"You guys are funny," she said.

"You'll have to pay a fare when you go through the Panama Canal, though." He knelt down and dug in his pocket, picked up her hand and placed the quarter in it. He carefully wrapped her fingers around the coin and let her hand plop into her lap. "This should take care of it."

"If you're gonna throw up, do it outside," I advised. "Crawl there if you have to." We could see her nipples poking out through her halter-top. I was tempted to reach over and pinch one, but didn't. I wasn't fucked up enough yet.

Loud banging on the open door, and Cindy's voice: "Police! This is a raid!" She banged on inside, uninvited. Smiling. Trendoids, posing in their expensive leather jackets, hair dyed rainbow colors and moussed up spiky, jerked around nervously looking for a way out, then relaxed. "How's the boy?" Cindy said.

"Don'tcha wanna say hey to your fiancée?" Albino asked.

"What happened to her?" Cindy asked, even sounding a bit worried.

"Lesbian love," Albino replied. "And Christian love, too."

"Where have you been keeping yourself?" Cindy asked me, ignoring Albino. She had on a denim vest with snaps in the front, a pair of cutoffs, and mirrored aviator's glasses. She could wear a burlap sack and still be the sexiest woman in any room.

"I've been around," I said.

"I tried calling, but your mother bitched me out. Told me to find people my own age to hang out with. Told me to stay the hell away from you and never call again. What do you have to say for yourself?"

"I love you, baby?" I offered.

Her face softened for a moment. "Don't make fun," she said. "Did you rat yourself out, or not?"

"One, two, three, four!" Albino said. And he jerked Bunni to her feet.

"I didn't say a word to Mom," I said.

"Your sister, Little Miss Empress," Cindy said. "Where is her highness? I have a few choice words for her."

"Catfight!" Dave shouted from the couch.

"You get moved in all right?" Cindy asked Dave, right before Bunni opened her eyes and released a full-lunged scream. It was unearthly. And it seemed like it went on for about ten minutes. "Jesus," Cindy commented.

And I guess that was the wrong word to say to someone who'd just been let out of the Christian Treatment Center for Wayward Teens. Bunni slapped her hands over her mouth and headed for the door.

"On the plants," I shouted after her, following to make sure she didn't vomit on the concrete, where it might leave a stain. Instead, she vomited on the garden of river stones and stunted bushes that my mother had been murdering for the past six months. Most of the puke was liquid, and went right through the stones, though a couple of unchewed pepperoni circles sat atop the mess.

I imagined myself as a paleontologist for a moment, wearing a pith helmet, picking up the pepperoni with shiny scientific instruments.

"Most curious, Sir Charles," I said to my flamboyantly mustachioed colleague.

"Quite," Sir Charles said back, puffing thoughtfully on a pipe carved from a monkey's ass.

Bunni hightailed it down the street. I ran after her. All that I knew was that I had to catch her before something bad happened. I used to run track, so had no problem overtaking her after about half a block, where I tackled her on a lawn. We rolled like strapped together logs and came to a stop in front of a leering cement troll. She was on top. Her hair enmeshed my face. She slid off me and sat up. I sat up and coughed up a nicotine-flavored tar ball.

"It's Congressman Andy Ireland," I said after I regained my breath, and rubbed the troll on its head. "How y'doin', Andy?"

"Who's Andy Ireland?" she asked me.

"Our congressman," I said. "Eighth congressional district, Florida. Just became a Republican because everyone likes Reagan so much. And who can blame them?"

"You're smart," she said, and leaned over like she was going to kiss me.

I grabbed her ears to stop her. "Bunni," I said. "You gotta stop kissing people just 'cause they tackle you."

"I know," she said, and stuck out that bottom lip. But this time it was sad, and not just pathetic sad either. I thought about what Cindy had told me, about her old man duking her.

We sat there for a moment or two longer, with me holding her by the sides of her head, and her staring at me with her big wet eyes. Then the old man who owned the dump, a dead ringer for the lawn troll, came out and yelled at us. "Get off my lawn!" he went, all indignant. He then headed into the shrubs to turn on his garden hose. I hopped to my feet, yanked Bunni to hers, and we dashed off the lawn. He shouted after us. "And don't come back!" I shouted back, "Ah, fuck you, you fucking old man!" I figured he needed that kind of pick-me-up. Hating kids was better than bathing in a tub of Ben Gay and having a Geritol high colonic shoved up your ass at the same time.

The geezer yelled back something, but by that time Bunni had tossed her arm around my shoulders and was giggling moronically in my ear. I put my arm around her waist like we were pals. Maybe we were. Closer to the truth was, we were in the same war on the same side, just in different trenches.

I walked her back to the party and escorted her through it to my room, past drunks of different flavors, stoners, jocks, preps. I turned on my dim lamp and pulled the sheet and blanket off the bed. "You don't have to go home to that son-of-a-bitch tonight," I said. She lay down on the bed, her head on my pillow, and stared up at me expectantly. "Go to sleep," I said. "No one will touch you. I'll be right here." I sat cross-legged on the floor next to the bed. In a few minutes, I heard her snore softly.

Albino poked his head in the door. He gasped out his relief that I wasn't fucking her.

"How could I?" I asked him.

"I see what you mean," he said, staring down at her. But he didn't see what I meant. He sat down next to me. We didn't say a word for a while. Then he said, "You know what your sister's doing?"

"Tell me," I said.

"You wanna take a guess?" he asked me.

"Not really. Quit being a cocktease," I said.

"Your neighbors? The ones with the little kidney-shaped pool? I take it they're snowbirds," Albino said. That meant that they only spent winters down in Florida.

"Yeah," I said. "Fucking old people. When the revolution comes, I'll shoot them myself."

"She convinced all the manly jocks to bust in over there and go swimming in their underwear. She's standing on the deck with her arms crossed, supervising them. They keep talking about tossing her in the pool, but they're too afraid of pissing her off to do it." Albino smiled at me in the dim light. "That grim fucker with the huge head and blond curly hair really your brother?"

"That's him. Sparky. Buster took all his scholarship money and bought a print shop with it. The print shop went bust in three months, so now Sparky's working as a waiter at the Athens Café up in Gainesville just so he has enough money to eat."

"Someday you guys are gonna get some real payback on that fucker," Albino said. He reached around under the bed.

"What're you doing?" I went, panicky.

"That's what I thought," Albino said. "*Playboy? Penthouse?*"

"Those are between the box springs and mattress. Don't wake Bunni," I said.

"What's this?" he asked, brandishing a spiral notebook. He took it over to the lamp and opened it. "Newspaper clippings?" He flipped through them. "They're all about convicts getting electrocuted working on powerlines."

"During thunderstorms," I said. I'd been keeping tabs on what I was sure were the local government's illegal execution policies.

"This is sick," Albino said appreciatively. "What else you got under there?"

"Nothing," I snapped.

He put the first notebook back and produced a second. Over at the lamp, he said, "Weird. Did you draw these?"

"Yeah," I said.

"This one's me," he said. "Holy shit, it's like a photograph. Except I'm glowing and floating. How come my hands and feet are like that?"

"You're nailed right in," I said. "It's based on a Goya painting of Christ. If you look into the detailing that I created in the dark, that's Poland burning black over your shoulder, and Israel on the other side. The crown of thorns is made out of nickels."

"You made me Christ?"

"King of the Jews," I said. "It says so right over your head."

He flipped the page. "This one has to be your dad."

"Fires of hell."

Paging along. "Look at Sissy. Is that a monkey looking over her shoulder?"

"Yeah, kinda like a Frida Kalo I saw once," I said. I rarely let anyone but Sissy look at my drawings. But now that someone else was looking at them, I didn't feel nervous at all. Or pissed off, like I did when Sissy entered me in the countywide art contest, and I won second place. *See, Cindy,* I wanted to say, *here's my precious secret, the one I didn't tell you.*

I yawned dramatically, went to my closet and pulled

out an old sleeping bag covered with pictures of pheasants. I unrolled it next to my bed and curled up on my side atop it.

The next morning when I awoke, the bed was empty. The pillow was all gunked up. The revelers had gone home.

I staggered around the house, observing the wreckage. Sparky had filled five green garbage bags already. "Look at this," he said, persnickety as fuck. "And this over here." He pointed out stains and hunks of glass, bottle caps, bits of pizza. Pizza. That rung a bell. I toddled out front.

A cat was gnawing on one of the pepperonis. When I got close, it hissed at me, protecting its feast. I felt a dizzy rage boil up inside me. I ran over and kicked it across the lawn. It slinked quickly away.

"What'd you do that for?" Sissy asked, bleary-eyed. She was standing in the doorway, wearing only a huge, rumpled tee shirt.

"I don't have to tell you everything," I said.

"Sure you do," she said with an easy smile.

"No I don't," I said, and pushed past her into the house.

Sarasota's Alright If You Like Geezers

The elderly female corpse at the wheel of the Cadillac Coupe de Ville committed murder thirteen times on a boiling August afternoon, driving while dead in the cool comfort of her luxury car, cruise control on. She smacked into five people waiting for the SCAT bus, then crashed through a Shell station, mowing down a motorcyclist in the process. Eventually, she ended up grill first through the pane glass outer wall of the Waffle House restaurant, shredding skin and organs with jagged glass missiles, the car tires spitting up grass as it tried to continue forward. Her driver's license had been renewed by mail.

I had the Suncoast section of the *Herald-Tribune* spread out across the front counter, reading the mass murder report, when the withered man with the badly fitted hair mop toddled in, walker first, his oxygen bottle dragging behind. The docs kept that well-insured fucker coked to the gills all the time, hooking him on legal heroin-equivalents so they could keep scamming him out of his lucrative insurance money. There was a geezer containment center on every other street corner in Sarasota awaiting those strung-out old people.

The old man slapped some coupons on the counter and said, "Get to work."

And was shocked when I laughed at him.

"What do you think is so funny?" he asked.

"'Get to work,'" I repeated, laughing. I picked up the coupons and studied them. They were two years expired. "Sorry, pops. These ain't no good." I shoved them back at him.

"I want to see your manager," he declared with a snort.

"Yeah," I said. "Me, too." I continued reading the paper, perusing for more electrocution-by-other-means stories.

A gnarled hand slapped the newspaper in front of my face. "Now!" he demanded. He was sucking the oxygen pretty hard through the tube in his nose. I wondered what kind of narcotics the geezer had on him. It didn't matter to me whether they were generics or not. I wasn't a pill snob.

"Now, what?"

That confused him. "What do you mean?"

"It doesn't seem to me that you're treating me with even a modicum of respect. Just saying 'please' might be a start," I said evenly.

That got him going, got those nostrils of his working

extra hard. He'd have to reach into the pocket of his safari jacket for his meds if I kept it up. Then he might drop those meds, accidentally, and I'd have to help him clean them up, nice guy that I am, because he obviously couldn't bend over. Not with that aluminum erector set propping him up. "Now you listen to me!"

"No," I said. I licked my finger and grandly flicked to the next page of the paper.

He slapped the counter again. I slapped it even harder. Then I hopped up and down like Yosemite Sam. "Consarn you, rabbit!" I shouted. "Great jumpin horny toads!" I stopped as suddenly as I'd started and went back to the paper, keeping a covert eye on him in case he had an infarction.

The restaurant was empty save for the two of us and Sissy, who was on the floor out in the dining room, biting her hand and shaking like she was having a seizure. I could feel him staring at me, enraged. Like a lot of stupid people who somehow manage to grow old, he thought that not dying young entitled him to respect. As far as I was concerned, there was no difference between a stupid young person and a stupid old one. "I have tomato sauce on my chin," I said, pretending to be reading. "Don't I?"

"Listen," the old man said, attempting reason. "I'm on a budget."

"And I'm not? How am I supposed to pay for your

meal when I'm making $3.10 an hour? Because if this 'manager' that you speak of finds expired coupons in the register, that's what I'm going to have to do," I said. I flicked to the next page. "And what are you doing in here if you're on a budget? Across the street at Winn Dixie they sell frozen pizzas for a quarter of the price we charge here. They taste better, too. Haven't you given up enough of your money over a long lifetime to rip-off organizations like this?" I glared over at him. "Well?"

"I don't have to take this from some young bum," he said. He clumped his way out the door. Sissy held it open for him.

After the door swung shut, she said, "You really laid into that one."

"If I ever end up like that, do me a favor and beat me to death with a tire iron." The phone rang. I let it ring a few times then picked it up. "Bee Ridge Pizza Hut, home of the Supreme Pan Pizza. My name is Jello. May I take your order?"

"Hi, Jello," Albino's voice went. "I'd like some glue to huff."

"Would you like that in a bag, or a la Carte?"

"Um, what would you suggest?"

"Shoving it up your ass," I said.

"I believe that would make it hard to defecate."

"Gimme that phone," Sissy said, and snatched it away from me. "Hi, sugar. This is Eden, the new waitress. I'm a 44 double D. Baby, I could love you all up." Then she said in her normal voice, "If you and Wayner aren't here on time, I'll take away Buzz's Valium stash. Then you'll be in a heap of trouble, boy." She listened, grimacing. "I don't care if Wayner saw a generalissimo on a stack of bales, you be here on time."

I heard Albino's voice going on and on.

She said, "No way," then hung up. "He wants to borrow your van. Wayner claims to have seen a bunch of bales floating in." Wayner lived in his mother's condo north of Siesta Key Beach. Bales floated in all the time. Reagan's drug war.

"No way," I said. "If the Coasties don't get them, the local pigs will. Pigs don't like indies. Pigs need their cut."

"They're coming over anyway," Sissy said.

"You talk to them," I said.

"I intend to." She headed back out to the dining area to continue setting up for the dinner shift, rolling silverware and topping off the salad bar.

I found another vehicular-homicide-by-geezer story in the paper. A certified grandpa in a Chrysler Imperial was cruising down Stickney Point Road at sundown. The late day glare blinded him to the girl heading home from the library on her bicycle. He clipped her, and she tumbled into the drainage ditch on the side of the road. Luckily, she wasn't too badly hurt. Yet. CG, upon hearing the noise, decided to stop the car, clunk it into reverse and go back to investigate. He figured he'd killed a squirrel, he told the paper. Then he heard another thump-thump while backing up. He'd run over the girl as she crawled out of the drainage ditch. He expressed his sorrow over the family's loss. And immediately went on to rant about how the girl shouldn't have been on the road, that her family was negligent for allowing her to be out so late at night, and so on. It was everybody's fault but his. The county prosecutor would probably cut a deal with the old fart.

I wadded up the paper and dropkicked it toward the break area, then poured myself a Mountain Dew, no ice, extra syrup. I chugged it down, along with a tiny white pill I'd stolen from my grandmother. I kept my stash in a green change purse that looked like a tiny rubber cunt. It had been a gift from Sarasota Savings and Loan after I opened my second savings account there—this time with no co-signer. Every time I'd go to a friend's house, I'd excuse myself and go to the master bathroom and thieve out of the medicine cabinet. It was a tense world. Moms and dads needed pharmaceuticals to get through the day. Reaganomics may have been a great deal for stockbrokers and other bandits fucking America up the ass, but it didn't do dick for working stiffs. The only drug I absolutely wouldn't steal was codeine. That shit made me sick.

I scraped down the make table, swept the floor, washed out the dough barrel, smoked a cigarette, drank more

Mountain Dew, swallowed another pill, accidentally set the trashcan on fire and had to slap the lid on it right quick before all hell broke loose, sprayed industrial Lysol all over the place to kill the burn stink, mopped the floors with Pine Sol for the same reason, and, while emptying out the trashcan in the dumpster, discovered that I could sense each individual strand of my hair. Even the two or three pubes around my dick tingled. "Oh, my," I went, talking to myself. "My oh my oh my oh my."

Cindy stood there staring at me. I thought that maybe she wasn't actually there, that I was imagining her. Because she looked better than any woman I'd ever seen.

"You're high," she said.

"You are so beautiful that I can't believe it," I said. She was beyond radiant. "Can I touch you? Can I? Can I?" Her Mercury Comet was parked next to my van. An old Charlie Brown pillow that I'd given her was in the back window, staring out at us dolefully. He had a hole in his neck and was bleeding gray stuffing.

She hovered over and put her arms around me. I still hadn't decided whether or not she was real. She took off my silly red uniform hat and ran her fingers through my hair. This was beyond intense. My tear ducts welled up. She smelled like wildflowers. She placed her lips near my ear and whispered, "What happened to you at the party the other night? You disappeared."

I closed my eyes. Each word was a flower petal drifting through me. I sighed.

"You smell like yeast," she said. They were the four most wonderful words I'd ever heard in my life. My grandmother! She had the greatest pills on earth. I had to get more.

"I love you," I said.

"Now I know you're wasted," she said, stepping back. "Listen, I have something I need to tell you..."

"You're liquid sunshine," I said, not listening to her. "You're the tide slipping across a sandbar in the moonlight."

"Oh my God," she went. Her free hand slipped up to her mouth. She dropped the hat and stared down at my crotch. She composed herself and reached into my pocket, pulling out my keys. Then she pulled me toward the van, unlocked the sliding door, and led me by the hand inside. It was as hot as a furnace. She shoved the door shut from the inside and rolled the windows down. Then she pushed me down to the floor, unzipped my pants, and yanked them and my briefs down to the knees. She pulled off her panties from underneath her dress and mounted me.

We lay there afterward sweating and panting, her leg tossed over me. I pulled up my pants. The best part of my high was gone, consumed by something better.

We kissed for a while. I'll be the first straight guy on earth to admit it, I love kissing. It's so tactile, so joyful. The best part of kissing is right before, as you close your eyes and taste her warm breath. The anticipation of things is always better than what really happens.

The van was still hot, so she got up and looked for something to wipe herself off with. She found the Zayre's shirt she had bought me stuffed behind the spare tire. She shook her head at me, then used it and put it back.

We unassed the van, and she left her panties behind accidentally on purpose.

"Do you really love me?" she asked when we were outside.

I took her hand in mine, thumbed her knuckles. "Yes," I said, too solemnly.

She threw the other hand in front of her mouth and tried to stuff a laugh back in.

I let go of her hand and stomped away. She chased after me. "Buzz! Buzz, I didn't mean it!"

I shook my head from side to side, my fists balled up. My happiness was gone now, replaced by my best friend— rage. I felt her hand on my shoulder. I shrugged it off.

"I'm sorry," she said. "I don't know why I laughed. I'm sorry. Please."

I wouldn't look back at her because I knew that if I did, I would forgive her. I took off in a jog and went around to the back door. I slammed it shut, and leaned my back against it. "I'm a chump," I said aloud.

Bang-bang-bang! "Buzz! C'mon, sweetie!" she hollered. Then I heard her mutter, "Temperamental little shit."

Albino came around the corner, zipping up his uniform smock. "Skyrockets in flight," he sang. "Afternoon delight." He tossed me my hat. I caught it and put it on. He smirked, incredulous. "Goddamn, man. If the van's a-rockin-! I brought the trashcan in with me. You trying to burn the place down again?"

"Did you look?" I asked, feeling a bit embarrassed, but really kind of proud of myself.

"I saw Cindy's head. Her hair actually. Whipping around," Albino said. "You're my hero, man. I'm having tee shirts made up with your graven image on them."

"What happened with the bales?" I asked him, changing the subject. I heard the bell attached to the front door ding-a-ling. I wasn't mad at Cindy anymore. I wanted to kiss her.

"Ah, that fucking Wayner. Thirty-year-old girly ass fucker who lives with his mom! There weren't any goddamned bales," Albino spat. "Drove all the way out to Siesta Key for nothing. He made me look at his mother's Hummel collection, the weirdo. He probably wants to fuck me in the ass."

"Is Buzz back here?" I heard Cindy ask.

Albino turned his head and grinned lustily at her.

"Forget Buzz. I've got all you need right here, baby."

"Don't make me smack you around," Cindy said.

"I'm here," I called out, still leaning against the back door. I drummed my fingers against it, looked down at my shoe-tops.

She pushed past Albino, who openly checked her out as her body swept across his. "Alan! Alan, get out here!" I heard my sister shout. I thought, *Alan? When did that happen?*

Cindy stopped in front of me. Her eyes were serious. She gently laid her hand across the side of my face, her fingertips touching my ear. Her thumb caressed my cheekbone. "I have something to say...hey, you're crying."

"No I'm not," I said. But then I realized I was.

Greedy and Pathetic

"How would you feel if it was me out in the parking lot?" Sissy asked me. "Putting out for some guy?"

"I don't know," I said. A hangover was creeping over my skull.

"What if that guy was in his 20's, like your *girlfriend*?"

"Stop hectoring me," I said. "You've harshed my mellow all to hell."

"Buzz, I have to stop you. I have to, because it's my job to stop you every damned time you try to do something stupid. Which is daily. I won't have you screwing up your life." She was sitting on the bed, her feet swinging.

"But I want her. And she wants me," I said. "Doesn't that count for something?"

"It's greedy and pathetic," Sissy said. We were in her room, listening to one of her records. Simon and Garfunkel. Feeling groovy.

"I feel kind of sick," I said. I was on the floor, hands clasped between my knees, head leaning against the bed frame.

"You're a dope," Sissy said. "She's using you. She gets off on how weird and pathetic you are. She doesn't really care about you."

"Quit calling me pathetic," I said. "And she does too like me. I'd swear to that on a stack of Bibles."

"You're an atheist," Sissy said. "What good would that do?"

"I'm an agnostic, thank you very much," I said. "So I can't take the chance that there may be a vengeful God out there in the ethers who wouldn't take kindly to me bullshitting on a stack of Bibles."

Sissy groaned. "Ugh! There are plenty of girls at school who'd date you if you got a haircut and stopped acting like a lunatic." *Stopped acting like a lunatic.* There it was again. Since I was a little kid, school counselors and teachers had been suggesting that I needed to see a shrink. As far as I was concerned, shrinks had one goal: to turn everyone on earth into a good company man. Then we could have an entire globe coated with glad-handing salesmen, beaten-down factory workers and fast food outlets and malls staffed by the living dead. The American Fucking Dream.

Plenty of girls? Who's the bullshitter now? I thought. "So what?" I said.

"'So what?' So they're your own age, that's what," Sissy said.

"So an asshole's an asshole, no matter the age."

The point was probably moot, as Rick Springfield, the soap opera star, would sing. Even before she said a word, I knew the real reason that Cindy had come to the Pizza Hut to see me. "Buzz, I came by to tell you I'm leaving tomorrow for New Hampshire," she said, wiping my tear away with her thumb. "Please, don't be sad." Then she began to cry.

I immediately started beating myself up for being stupid enough to fall for her. "Don't pay any attention to me," I said. "I'm just a kid."

"No you're not," she said, and went on to blubber all sorts of irrelevant bullshit to stroke my ego. How I was special and not like other people and *you know*. Bullshit. And, if there's one thing I won't stand for, it's being complimented. Having a con man father will do that for you. The year before, I'd won second prize at the county art fair for a self-portrait that was based on one by Van Gogh. The photo in the paper the next day showed a miserable, flea-bitten train wreck teenager being handed a piece of paper that may have been covered with shit, the way he was daintily pinching it. A few minutes after receiving the award, I dropped it in a nearby trashcan.

I marched away from Cindy, punched out, and snapped at my sister, "You coming, or what?" She was standing next to the salad bar, yakking with Albino. She gave him a peck on the cheek, punched out and came along with me.

And now the lecture.

A smack on the back of my head. "Are you listening to me?"

"Yeah, yeah," I went. "I'm stupid, you're smart, and the world's rotating off its axis." I got up. "I'm taking a shower. I stink." I left her room before Art Garfunkel started sermonizing about what to do when I'm weary and feeling down. That curly headed fucker.

Back in my room, Sparky was packing up to go back to college. He folded his clothes in neat, precise squares so that they lay down perfectly atop one another. *What a prig*, I thought.

"Have you seen my Susan B. Anthony dollars?" he asked. He never said *hello* or *how-you-doing*.

"Not lately," I said. I grabbed a pair of jeans and a pocket tee shirt out of my bureau, a new pair of briefs and mismatched tube socks. "So what's college like?" I asked him.

"Can you be more precise?" he asked, not looking up, just folding and folding.

"Fuck it," I said, and left the room. The guy was my brother and I didn't know dick about him, or him me. Every time I spoke to him, he pissed me off with his snotty, emotionless, I'm-smarter-than-you pose. And he was studying mathematics, trying to quantify the universe, like all of life's problems could be solved with an algorithm. As far as I was concerned, he had all the humanity of the cardboard shipping container that he was filling up with his perfectly square clothes.

I took a quick shower and changed. Then I went back in my room and cranked up my cheap ass, all-in-one stereo, dropping the stylus on some Roach Motel. "I Hate the Sunshine State" segued into "Brooke Shields Must Die." Sparky decided to leave, sniffing his disapproval at me on the way out. He was into all progressive rock, the kind of shit that goes on for twenty minutes with important guitar and organ riffs blooping and whirling. After "My Dog's into Anarchy," I turned the stereo off and locked the door. I rolled under the sheets, and tried to cut some Z's.

I was asleep for only a few moments, it seemed, but now it was dark and someone was beating on the door. I clicked on the light. "Yeah, yeah," I said. I figured it was Sparky wanting to get in. When I opened the door, Cindy was standing there. "How'd you get past the hall monitor?" I asked her.

"Your sister? Or your brother? He answered the door, so it was easy to get in." She sauntered past me. "So this is your hovel." She rotated around. "Why aren't there any posters taped to the walls?"

"That would mean that I live here by choice. I'm an inmate," I said. I closed the door behind her.

She put a restraining hand on my chest. "No hanky

panky," she said. "I came here to tell you that I'll be back. I don't know when, but I will. Are you going to wait around for me, or what?"

"Since you're the only woman who's ever shown the slightest interest in me, why not?"

"That's not much of an answer."

"I'm 17," I said. "It's the best I can do." I sat down on the bed and she sat next to me. She took my hand in hers. She patted it some. I heard a car pulling into the driveway. It was Buster's. I could tell because the engine knocked, pinged and sputtered horribly. "That's my asshole father," I said. "Where'd you park?"

"On the street, a couple of doors down," she said. She turned toward me and hurried up her speech. "I always liked you, with your sharp comments about everything, your smirky cynicism. I only wanted to use your van that day. But when you stood there begging for me not to hurt you ..."

The door swung open. I'd forgotten to lock it. "Get her out of here!" Sissy hissed.

"Calm down," I said. "It's Buster. He'll be proud of me for being with a real woman, the fuckhead."

"Mom's with him," she said. "You remember her, don't you? Saint Lola of the Cuyahoga?" She slapped off the light and quickly swung the door shut. We were left in darkness.

"So," I whispered, "I guess you'll be going out the

window."

She whispered back, "It won't be the first time." Her voice was all quivery and strange. I put my arm around her. She said, "I didn't want it to end like this."

I took her hand and walked her over to the window. I yanked the shade up and cranked open the window, popped out the screen like I'd done a million times before. "Buzz is asleep," I heard Sparky say. "He passed out as soon as he got home from work. He's been working too hard, I think." Well, mother*fucker!* The stiff could actually lie. And lie for me. It was touching.

I placed my hands on Cindy's waist, but didn't kiss her. We stood in my parents' house, the two of us dusted by moonlight filtered through the filthy window. I wanted to etch her into my memory. On a good day, I can close my eyes and see her just as she was, so goddamned long ago.

And then I helped her out the window. Once her feet touched the ground, she pecked me on the cheek. "Don't go changing," she said, and was gone, jogging off into the night. I stuck my head out the window and listened to her cheap clogs clacking the sidewalk. Her car started up. I listened to it drive away. She hadn't bothered to say the word. Goodbye.

"This is what you get," I said and hauled off and slugged myself in the face. I fell to the ground. It didn't hurt yet, but it would soon enough. I picked myself up and put the screen back in place. Then I got into bed. I rolled onto my side and gritted my teeth, my face beginning to pulse with pain, my eyes pinched shut, and growled, "Never again, never again, never again." I fell asleep like that.

Sissy shook me awake. "Did she hit you?"

"No," I said. "I hit myself."

She gave me this look like she didn't even know me. "Jesus. You should be committed. Do yourself a favor and skip looking in any mirrors this morning," Sissy said. Her face softened. "Cindy's gone for good, isn't she?"

"Yep," I said. "Happy?"

"No," Sissy said. She sat down next to me, put her hand on my shoulder. Sparky's bed was empty. Hospital corners. "Yeah, he's gone, too. You should have seen him acting his ass off last night. Sometimes he can actually do a pretty good impression of a human being. You owe him big time." She slipped her hand down to my heart. "Can you see well enough to drive?"

"Why?"

"I figured we'd go up and visit the grandparents." Sissy loved the two old coots, and so did I. We spent our summers with them when we were little kids. I had learned my contempt of authority from Pop, who was a hardcore socialist and union man. America was one big scam, founded by rich people who didn't want to pay taxes, and run by the sons of those assholes, who would juice the last ounce of sweat out of you then kick you into your grave, he told me time and again. The old lady was a closet fine artist, and totally nuts. She used to be a professional roller skater back in the 1920's, when the old man was a professional boxer. She ended up selling shoes, and he ended up a letter carrier. They were both so wonderfully bitter, but in completely different ways. His bitterness steamed out of every pore of his body. Hers was subtler. She was a pill-popper, just like me. Or rather, I was just like her.

Pop would be just the tonic I needed. If anyone had any stories about how debasing and horrible love is, it would be him. "Let's go," I said.

The vacuum cleaner started up. I could hear Mom humming over the top of it. Her enraged hum.

"You better handle her," I said. "She's in a snit today."

"Yeah, she might not let us go if she sees your face," Sissy said.

Something clanked around in the vacuum and Mom shut it down. "Hey!" Mom shouted. "Where'd this bottle cap come from?"

My heart jumped. Sissy smirked. "It's all in the tone of your voice," she said. "Listen and learn, young Skywalker."

"Yeah," I said. "Go get her, Yoda. Deny everything."

"Don't be cute," Sissy said. "It's your ass I'm saving, too." She left the door partially open, so that I could listen.

"Do you kids hear me?" Mom shouted. "Miller! Nobody drinks Miller in this house!"

"Remember Sparky's friend?" Sissy said to her.

"What about'm?" Mom went.

"The fat guy, who couldn't move his neck?" Sissy said. "The one who said he could hypnotize you into eating an onion and thinking it was an apple?"

"You're gonna tell me it was his beer?" Mom said, unbelieving. *We're dead*, I thought. "That the bottle cap has been under the couch for a year?"

"Who else?" Sissy asked innocently.

"Did you kids have a party while we were gone?" Mom asked. *God*, I thought, *the old lady has us this time*.

"With Sparky here?" Sissy asked, with that are you kidding tone to her voice.

"Okay," Mom said. "Dumb question." Mom's brain grinding away. I could picture it. Mom's suspicious look. Sissy standing there with her innocent schoolgirl smile, with a pinch of you're stupid-if-you-don't-believe-me tossed in. "So that fat kid was sitting here drinking beer while we were all in bed? Is that it?"

"I got up in the middle of the night to go pee and saw him. Sparky was already in bed. I didn't want to say anything to get Sparky in trouble," Sissy said.

"Did you tell Sparky?"

"Nuh-uh," Sissy went. "Because I knew he'd tell you and get himself in trouble."

"You think you have all the answers, don't you Miss Tish?"

"Okay, *don't* believe me!" Sissy screamed. "Make something bad up about me if it makes you feel better! Go ahead and see if I care!" Cue the waterworks.

"Okay, okay," Mom said after a second or two. "Calm down. I believe you."

I shook my head. Incredible.

A few minutes later, Sissy came back in, wiping away a self-induced tear. "Put your shoes on," she said. "We're gone."

Police Story

There are two ways to get to Nalcrest from Sarasota.

One way takes you along the coast on US 41 up by Tampa to Brandon, then you take a right on State Route 60 and drive through phosphate mining country, where you can witness capitalism at its absolute finest. Are those glowing slurry pits radioactive? Yes, they are. The best thing about this route is stopping in Gibsonton, about halfway up the coast. It's where all the circus and sideshow freaks go to retire.

The other route takes you out toward the middle of the state. You head out on State Route 72 through Arcadia, home of the G. Pierce Wood State Mental Hospital. Arcadia's a great place to get lynched, too. A few years after our trip, little Ricky Ray, the 14-year-old inbred hemophiliac redneck that caught HIV from infected blood platelets, was burned out of his house and chased from town, "FAGGOT" spray-painted on the ruins of his family's shack.

We took the Arcadia route.

After Arcadia, you turn left and head north, where there's nothing and more nothing. Most people don't know how ugly Florida is away from the coasts. They think Florida's all sunshine and beaches and bikinis. The meat of Florida is flat, featureless and stripped clean, thanks to cattle ranching, phosphate mining, overdevelopment, drained wetlands, Mediterranean fruit flies and citrus chancre.

I stepped on the gas. The road rushed under us, an asphalt river. Everything sped up. Grass stalks grew up and swallowed road signs. Children standing on the side of the road transformed into old-timers. My head roaring, metallic squeals, blue smoke behind us. Two hours equals 140 miles. We ventured through Florida's secret, untouristy middle, bursting with Brahmin cattle and stretches of two-lane highway, greenish brown prairies teaming with insects, disease, cowshit. Turkey buzzards scudding atop hot updrafts a mile high.

A wall of rain appeared a half-mile ahead of us, and we slammed into it at eighty miles per hour. I clunked the windshield wipers to life. The one on Sissy's side uprooted itself from its metal arm and flopped crazily before flying away. What remained behind etched a semicircle, shrieking like a smacked baby. We emerged from the wall of water into the blinding sun, humidity fuming through the van.

We stopped for gas and a replacement wiper in Lake Placid. There was no lake that I could detect. Sissy and I took turns in the washroom. When I emerged, I found a local boy chatting her up. He was shirtless and shoeless, wearing a pair of chewed up cut-offs. Sun blisters dotted his broad back. I heard him say, "You raht purty," like we were trapped in some Burt Reynolds car chase flick. I paid the attendant and bought a glass bottle of orange Fanta out of one of those old-fashioned machines, the kind where you have to open a little door and yank the bottle out. I decapped it and handed it to Sissy. "This got to be your brother," the boy said.

"Am I purty, too?" I asked.

"Be nice," Sissy said.

"Boy, don't make me kick your ass in front of your sister," he said.

I felt a short adrenaline thrill surge through me. I wanted him to kick my ass. I took half a step forward before Sissy's hand flew up to my chest. She said, "You should see the other guy," to the local yokel.

He studied my face. My self-inflicted wound had turned terrifically purple. "Shit," he said, and spat on the ground. "Your brother do have a little crazy to him. I can tell." He smiled at us. Blackened teeth. "You folks have a nice trip." He went inside to yammer with the attendant.

Sissy swigged the Fanta and handed it to me. "He was telling me that everybody out here's broke," she said. "All the orange trees had to be burned."

"What happened?"

"Who the hell knows? The same thing that always happens to dirt farmers, I guess. Bugs, disease. Bad gets worse. Let's book," she said. We got into the van and revved it up. Sissy slapped her sandaled feet up on the dash. I handed her the bottle, and we slipped out of town.

I clicked on the radio and slid the dial around until I found some good, old-timey, wrath of God music. *Never let the devil get the upper hand on you.* It faded in, and faded out. As it faded out for the last time, I heard the faint gasp, "Wi-dow maker! Widder ma-ker!"

One desolate tourist trap advertised itself on roadside signs for twenty-five straight miles. In Burma Shave fashion, we were informed that it had had alligator wrestling, orange juice, citrus candy and hunks of cypress that looked like famous dicks from history and TV. When we got to the place, it appeared to be a two-acre ranch tangled with barbed wire, and littered with tree stumps. We zipped by. A sign told us to go back, that we'd missed it. We gave the sign the bird.

A Donald Duck orange juice sign loomed ahead, and we caught our first whiff of the vomity orange stench of boiling orange pulp becoming concentrate. We could only escape it by speeding. I zoomed past a state trooper. "Oh, shit!" I went. He didn't move. I dropped the van down into second anyway and let out the clutch. The tranny screamed out in pain. The empty Fanta bottle rolled forward and clunked into the center console. The trooper was receding in the rearview. I shifted back into third.

"Guess he got his quota," Sissy said, right as the pig's blues flashed on.

"We don't have any pot in here, do we?" I asked, panicky.

"Shit!" Sissy went. "Oh, fuck!" She rummaged around under the seat as I pulled over. The trooper flew past us and away.

"Jesus, I almost had a heart attack," I said, pulling back out onto the highway.

Sissy waved a pair of panties at me. "Yours?" she asked.

"Just to snuggle and sniff," I said.

"She wrote a New Hampshire address on them with a laundry marker," Sissy said, stretching them out. "Right on the crotch. Very tasteful."

"I guess she thought that would make it harder to toss the address," I said.

"She was wrong," Sissy said, and whipped them out the window.

I slammed on the brakes. "What'd you do that for?"

"Buzz, if we don't get out of here soon, I'm gonna puke," Sissy said, pulling her tee shirt up to her nose. The concentrate smell was overwhelming. "We're on a highway, dumbass," her muffled voice went. "Forget the panties."

I pulled the van over and started to open the door.

"If she really cares, she'll write you!" Sissy shouted through her shirt. "Let's go! Go!"

I opened the van door a crack and vomited onto the pavement. It was all orange fizz. I slammed the door shut and put the van in gear, shuttling out onto the highway without looking behind me. A truck horn blasted blowing past, zigzagging the van. Sissy leaned out her window and puked, spitting a couple of times for good measure. Then she opened the glove compartment and produced a couple of tissues. We wiped, wadded and tossed.

Up ahead, we saw a migrant family kneeling on the side of the road next to a ruined antique pickup truck, hands on heads. A state trooper peered through the driver's side window. Dark shades and Smokey the Bear hat. Heavy pistol.

"Good thing we're not dark," I said.

"Or dirt poor," Sissy added.

I slowed up and rubbernecked at the poor people who were getting shaken down. I knew what my grandfather would say when I told him about it. "Great country," he'd say. "Land of the free. Home of the brave."

Our queasiness subsided as we got away from the boiling pulp. We pulled into the parking lot of a Burger Chef and went inside to eat. We'd become accustomed to eating after puking our guts out.

We took our crap burgers and crap fries and crap fizzing sugar water over to a crappy, but cleanish, table. (Only one or two houseflies.) Through the window, Lake Wales bustled the best it could. During Lent, the city put on a daily passion play in which Jesus got lynched over and over and over, until the ACLU put an end to public funding for it. Jesus would have to be killed by corporate sponsorship forever after.

"Which ring of hell is this?" I asked Sissy, dunking the last of my fries into the dollop of ketchup on my burger wrapper.

"Fifth," she replied. "Wife beaters, sleazoids, cops. You know. The people who live in our neighborhood." Our brother'd left a copy of Dante's *Inferno* in my room after Christmas break. We'd both fallen in love with it.

"So tired," I said, wiping my mouth with a paper napkin embossed with corporate mascots Burger Chef and Jeff. "I slept all night and feel like I didn't sleep at all."

Sissy slurped the rest of her drink through the straw. "You want me to drive?" She popped off the plastic lid and tapped an ice chunk into her mouth.

"Nah, we're only a few miles away now," I said. "I'll be okay." I didn't feel okay. I felt like digging a hole and crawling inside.

"Buck up, little buckaroo," Sissy said. She tapped out a couple of cigarettes, lit them both in her mouth, and handed me one. She had switched back to Winstons.

I took a long drag, tilting my head back. I exhaled and said, "How could I fall for her so quickly? I guess I fell for her a long time ago. Way back when she was hired. It's just that consummating it ..."

"Consummating it?" Sissy shouted. Then quietly, leaning over the table, squinting at me. "Consummating? You slept with her?" She tapped out some ashes into the aluminum ashtray.

"I made love to her," I said. "Yeah."

"Listen to you. 'Made love.' Yeesh," Sissy went. "Really, though? You did?"

"Yeah," I said, cautiously. "What's the big deal?"

"Have you told anybody? Other than me?"

"No," I said.

"Don't," she said. "Don't tell anyone."

"Why?" I asked.

"You'll understand someday. Take it from me, don't tell a soul," Sissy said, shaking her head no. "Keep it ... I don't know ... *sacred* somehow." She stubbed out her cigarette.

I stared across the table at her. She was dead serious. It was wounding to me, somehow. "Okay," I said. I did anything she told me to. I couldn't remember a time when I didn't. It seemed like I'd been obeying her since before either of us was born.

We went back out to the van and hopped in. I pulled

out onto SR 60 and sped toward the grandparents' place. "You didn't have to toss the panties, though," I said.

"What're you gonna do when you go to college next year and you don't have me watching you all the time? Are you gonna be this stupid?" she asked me.

"I'm just saying," I said. "And who says I'm going to college?" I'd already half-decided to get a job as a lineman for the county after I graduated. Lightning, sparks. Or maybe take the assistant manager job Chuck was waving at me, "as soon as you turn 18." Another idea of mine was to go to Louisiana and get a job working on an oilrig, and sabotage the oil industry from the inside.

"I do," Sissy said.

I leaned forward onto the wheel and sighed. *That settles that*, I thought. "I sure could use a pick-me-up," I said.

"Plenty of that in the medicine cabinet where we're going," Sissy said.

Working Men Are Pissed

Nalcrest is the retirement village for the National Association of Letter Carriers. The center of the village is shaped like a wheel, with a bingo hall as the hub. Near the bingo hall stands a patina statue of a postman holding a letter. When I was a little kid, I imagined it as the village on *The Prisoner*, with a huge rubber ball filled with cancelled stamps and dead letters ready to grab me if I tried to make a run for it. "I will not be stamped, mailed, delivered, signed-for, insured, weighed or ZIP-coded!"

All the old postmen hung out at the post office, waiting on their mail, discussing post office business, comparing and contrasting the old Post Office Department with the new-fangled U.S. Postal Service. And ZIP codes, hah! Who needs 'em?

The apartments were all lined up in a single row on a single floor and were attached by outside sidewalks. Many postal retirees had taken a ration of pride in their places, planting their own bushes and flowers, or putting out flamingos and other statuary. Pop would have none of that. He wouldn't waste money on frippery. He was a Great Depression survivor, and knew that money could disappear in an instant. As a result, he lived frugally. My sister and I had learned a different lesson from hyperinflation and having Buster as a father.

My grandparents toddled out of their apartment to greet us. Grandmother made a big show of kissing each of us. Sissy and I were only 5 foot 7, but we towered over the old lady, who seemed to grow shorter each time we visited. Pop shook my hand and nodded.

"Father, look at that, such a big van!" Grandmother said, as if I'd built the thing with my own two hands.

Pop shrugged. "A van's a van," he commented grimly.

"It only seems big 'cause you're getting so small," Sissy said, patting Grandmother on the head.

"Everything except my nose and ears," Grandmother replied. "They just keep growing and growing." Then she got that look at on her face, the same one I got on my face, the same one Sissy got on her face, the same one our mother got on her face, the one we got when we're about to say something peculiar and a little cruel. "Warned your mother about that. But she won't listen. Soon enough, it'll happen to her, though. She'll get teeny-tiny with a great big nose. Hee-hee-hee."

We went inside, and Grandmother took me out back

to the porch to show me the painting she was working on. It was a rendering of an empty tomato vine. I thought I might be able to reach into the painting, it glistened so. The vine was like a blood vessel just about to burst. Around the vine, the grass was all brown and dead. An open empty tomato can lie rusting on the ground. Tiny bugs marched across the tomato blood vessel.

"Sometimes your mother tells me that, with your temper, she's afraid that you're too much like your father. But you're nothing like him. You're like us. Me, your mother, your sister. Yep." That look swept across her face. "You're just one of the girls. Hee-hee-hee."

Sissy came out of the bathroom and walked over to us. "Don't you have to go to the bathroom," Sissy asked me, "after that long ride?"

I looked at her like, *are you nuts?*

She looked back at me, her eyes saying, *go partake, you dope.*

Oh yeah. Silly me.

I stepped across the plastic runners, past Pop with his feet up. He was reading the sports section of the *Plain Dealer,* which he had mailed down to him from Cleveland by his brother Charlie, with whom he was not on speaking terms.

I heard Sissy snap, "But where are the tomatoes on the vine? Why paint an empty vine? I don't get it."

149

Pop said, "I've been saying the same damn thing. Not that it does any good."

I closed the door and carefully slid open the medicine cabinet. Oh my god. A fabulous pharmacopeia, mostly of the mood altering variety. I dug my green savings and loan coin cunt out of my pocket and tapped out a few from each bottle. Then I peed, flushed the toilet, washed my hands, popped a smiling blue pill, and went back out.

Sissy and Grandmother had gone off to the kitchen to prepare The Dinner of Many Separated Courses. Pop dropped the newspaper and said, "There's a ballgame on." Pop loved baseball; before becoming a postman, he had been a first basemen in the Cleveland Indians minor league system, (as well as a Gold Gloves boxer). I pulled out the volume knob on the set, and clunked the UHF dial over to channel 17. The top, middle and bottom of the screen were blue, red and green haze, but it looked like the Braves were playing the Cubs. The camera zoomed in on Harry Caray, who was in the opposing broadcasters' booth. "That old drunk got another job?" I went. Harry'd been fired by the White Sox a year or two before.

"Hey, easy," Pop said. "You happen to be watching the game with an old drunk. Now get me a beer, boy."

I went out to the porch where they had their second refrigerator, which had nothing in it but beer, bologna slices with the red wrapper rings, a loaf of Wonder bread, a nearly empty jar of French's yellow mustard, and a half-eaten five-pound block of government cheese. I pulled out a beer, popped it, and took it over to the old man. "You want me to get you a cigar?" I knew where he kept them.

"Nah, she don't let me smoke inside no more," Pop said. It was like, *modern times, who can figure?* "Now take your swig." It was a long-standing tradition. I took a big gulp, and handed him what was left.

"You're gonna get drunker'n me this afternoon," Pop commented with that oh-ho-ho expression.

I plopped down on the couch and slipped off my Chucks. I watched the game. It was some kind of awful. The only highlight was a Dale Murphy homerun. Six beers later, I was feeling mellow. So was Pop. He said, "You need a haircut."

"You offering to pay?" I asked.

"You look like a hippie," he said.

"I ain't no hippie," I said, maybe too sharply. Punks and hippies didn't get along. My junior year English teacher was an unreconstructed hippy, all full of himself. He and his much greater generation of deadbeat geniuses had defeated the powers that be and ended the Vietnam War, he would tell us all the time with pride. One day, I raised my hand, probably the first and last time I did that in that fuck-all school.

"Yes, Mr. Pepper," he went, all snotty.

"How long did it take, exactly, to end that war?" I asked.

"What do you mean?"

"I mean, how many years did it take for you to defeat those evil, evil people at the Pentagon? Six months? A year? Two years?"

"Um," he went, looking a little sheepish.

"How about twelve years, give or take a few," I said. Then I pasted that look on my face. "Gosh, old timer. I'd say there's nothing your generation can't do. Given time." I went on to accuse the hippies of getting Nixon elected. That did it. I had to go down to the principal's office. She was a sister from a teaching order in Elyria, Ohio, probably middle-aged, though you really couldn't tell with those uptight religious types. She went on about how she let me in the school ahead of other students because my father was such a great guy. *He's a bullshit artist,* I thought. *He snowed your ass good, you bitter old maid.*

I hated the pious dump, and the prissy fucks that matriculated there. For a while, I had hung out with a bunch of kids who called themselves The Group. I played Iago with them, whispering in their ears, making them fight. Eventually they caught on and threw me out, and even made some feeble attempts to terrorize me.

I had made a few actual friends who hated that school as much as I did. One guy paid me to take his GED for him so he could get the fuck out and go work for his dad's golf course lawn cutting service. Then there was this guy I'd met in Moral Guidance. We were supposed to introduce ourselves to someone in the class we didn't know, and then say something to the rest of the class about our new friend. He had me announce that he was a hardcore alcoholic and into snuff films. Me and him shared some quality time down in the principal's office.

My jaw muscles were sore and my teeth ached. I'd gotten myself all worked up. I needed another happy pill. I got Pop another beer, took a piss and popped another pill.

"Dinner's ready," Sissy said when I walked out of the bathroom. Pop and I sat down at the table. I had to scoot into the space between the table and the wall, and slip into the chair without pulling it out. Pop slid into a chair butted against the china cabinet.

"How're the Indians doing?" I asked him.

"Are you kidding?" he went. Other than Len Barker's perfect game during the strike year, there hadn't much to get excited about.

Sissy delivered a serving dish heaped with heavy potato dumplings. Then she brought out a stick of butter on a dish. Then salt and pepper. Grandmother always sent out the food like this, in illogical and haphazard stages.

Twenty minutes later, corn on the cob arrived.

Five minutes after that, some rolls appeared.

Ten minutes later, Sissy brought out some gravy. We poured the gravy over the potato dumplings and ate them.

"Mother," Pop said. "You okay in there?"

"Sure, sure," she replied. "Hold your horses."

A crash in the kitchen startled us. Sissy and I got up as quickly as we could. Grandmother was on the floor, and the roast had slid across the linoleum and spattered against the wall.

"Oh, my," Grandmother said. "Oh, me." We helped her to her feet and two brown prescription bottles dropped out of opposing pockets of her housecoat. One Dexamyl, the other Elavil. It was like that book I had read about the Lurps, army psychos in Vietnam, who always carried two pockets of pills. One pocket would take you down the road, the other would smooth the way. Sissy and I each took an arm and toted her to the bedroom and placed her on the bed.

"Maybe we should take her to the hospital," Sissy said.

"It's too late for that," Grandmother went. "Oh, too, too late. Darkness falls." And at that, she snorted loudly and dropped off to sleep, snoring like a chainsaw.

"Maybe not," I said. We tiptoed out.

"Pills," Pop commented, still sitting there. "I should flush 'em down the toilet."

"They'd just give her more," Sissy said with a slight shrug.

"Let me see if I can do something with that roast," I said and crept into the kitchen like I might startle the thing. I knelt down and forked it back onto the metal tray using a serving fork that had landed nearby. "Let's test that you-could-eat-off-it theory," I muttered, and took it out to the table. I cut Pop off a hunk and plopped it on his plate. He dug right in. Sissy and I did the same. "I smell something burning."

"The green beans!" Sissy shouted, and leapt up. She came back with a bowl of burnt green beans. We ate those, too.

I spent as long cleaning up as Grandmother and Sissy had spent preparing the feast. Every pot and pan was greasy or had food welded to it. I scrubbed everything in the miniature, one-basin sink and balanced the assemblage of pots, pans, serving containers and utensils atop a dishrag. It looked like a twenty-car pileup.

"Your turn," Sissy said, standing behind me.

"My turn?" I went.

"I heard her moaning and had to go in there," Sissy said, hands on hips. "Now she's asking for you."

I dried my hands on my pants and slipped carefully

into the bedroom, which was dimly lit by a bulb glowing in an old lamp in the corner.

"Come closer," Grandmother said, weakly.

"Okay," I said and sat on the side of the bed.

She took my hand and held it over her heart. "These could be the last beats of my heart. I'm very old, you know. And I wanted to tell you something. Lean down so I can whisper it in your ear." I leaned down. "You were always my favorite." It was kind of touching, really. I could feel my eyes growing wet for the old lady. And while my head was still down there, the chainsaw revved up again, almost blowing out my ear.

When I left the room, Sissy was standing there, hands in pockets, shifting from foot to foot, shaking her head knowingly. "She tell you you're her favorite?"

"Yeah. I guess she told you the same thing?" I went, wiping away a tear.

"Yeah, she told me how *you* are her favorite!" Sissy smiled like a wonderful practical joke had been played on both of us. "You gotta love that old lady. She's totally nuts." We both laughed. Hee-hee-hee.

Sissy and I stayed up late playing Crazy Eights and drinking Pop's beer atop the creaky, thin bed we'd pulled out of the sofa. The next morning, we opened our eyes at the exact same moment, smelling bacon and eggs. Our nose tips were touching. We scooted up and realized we were holding hands. We quickly let go of each other and slid to opposite sides of the bed, coughing. It wouldn't have bothered us before or after—we knew we had a deeper relationship than most brothers and sisters, no sexuality involved—but teen years, you know.

"Come in here and eat," Grandmother hollered. Everything was burnt. Pop didn't seem to notice and dug right in.

I snapped a piece of bacon in half. Ashes dotted my plate. I decided to excuse myself and go to the bathroom.

After I finished up, I thought about popping something from that wonderful cabinet, but decided to start the day straight and feel my way forward from there. I washed up a bit and deodorized my pits. In the mirror, I watched myself mouth, "Never felt better."

"You didn't eat nothing," Grandmother said when I came out.

"Sure I did. Look at my plate," I said.

Pop finished up and dropped his napkin onto his plate. "Let's go, boy." I guessed the gals would handle the dishes.

We walked outside into the blowtorch day. Pop sang as we strolled down to the barbershop. "They have taken untold millions that they never toiled to earn, but without our brain and muscle not a single wheel could turn. We can break their haughty power—gain our freedom when we learn that the Union makes us strong! Solidarity forever, solidarity forever, solidarity forever, for the union makes us strong!" He puffed on a Hav-a-Tampa, and hummed the parts he'd forgotten over the years. No doubt about it, Pop was a commie. Politically, I'd flirted with both major parties, then ended up being a kind of libertarian, since I disliked the government. Later, I found that I really hated big business. So I wasn't much of a libertarian, I guess. The only party that I had ever really wanted to join was the Black Panthers. When I was a little kid, they were on TV all the time. I wanted a pair of wraparound shades and a beret. I wanted to shout, "Kill whitey!" I was all for killing whitey. I had to sit at the dinner table with him every night. I imagined showing up one day with my brothers and sisters and pointing out The Man sitting there gulping down mashed potatoes and swilling his Red, White and Blue. They'd drag him away and toss him in a traveling cage on wheels, then put him on trial for his hate crimes. At some point during my dinnertime daydream, The Man would catch me giggling and whack me on the back of the head. He always suspected that when we were laughing, we were laughing at him. He was usually right.

About once a year, I take an instant dislike to someone. It's something about that person, their mien, that turns my stomach. We entered the barbershop, and I immediately had that feeling about the second barber, the one whose chair was empty. He had a pinched-up face, like someone had taped a dog turd under his nose twenty years ago and he'd never removed it, except to maybe freshen it with new dog turd. His black hair was slicked back tightly, as if it was wired to the base of his skull. He wore a pair of glasses that magnified his tiny rat eyes to bulging. I wanted to punch the fucker in the guts five seconds after I saw him. He wasn't much bigger than I was. I could probably take him on pure rage.

He peered over at me coolly. *Kick him in the balls!* screamed my brain. "Next," came out of his contemptuous slit of a mouth.

"Go ahead," Pop said. He said he wanted to wait for the other barber.

"I do, too," I said, glaring over at my new enemy.

"Ah, go over there," Pop said, giving me a push. "He can't do too much damage."

"Him wants to sit down, yes," he said to me. "Let's see what we can do." He spun me round in the chair until I faced the mirror, then almost strangled me when he put the tissue around my neck. "Such a nice head of hair. Too bad him doesn't like to comb it, hmm?" A newspaper photo of Old Sparky, the Florida state electric chair, was taped to the mirror. A well-thumbed paperback edition of *Thuvia, Maid of Mars* sat next to a wax paper cup brimming with orangeade, and a blue-fluid jar filled with combs.

He waved a scissor at my head, wondering where to dig in. Then he started cutting, at the same time trying to make small talk by asking, seriously, "Him has played D and D before, hmm?" He continued on by telling me all sorts of tidbits about himself that weren't interesting to anyone but himself. He didn't have a girlfriend. He had problems meeting other people. Even role-playing games weren't helping out. He explained the stupid dice, and talked about his goddamned tenth level elf, or some shit like that. I caught a look at my face in the mirror. Pure rage.

I tried to tune him out, but his voice was too atonal to be tuned away. It was like a cut-rate violin being played with an unresined bow. *This is what hell would be like,* I thought. He lathered up my neck and took a straight razor to it. Were the Tarzan books better than the John Carter of Mars books? He answered yes and no and went on to explain. I prayed for him to hit a major artery.

Now he was swiping my neck with a talcum-powder brush. The long national nightmare was coming to a close. He swung me around and held up a hand mirror so I could observe the back of my neck in the big mirror. The rat bastard had given me a fantastic haircut. Perfect. I looked like a regular citizen now. I'd blend right in with all my fascist school colleagues. I was Harry Reasoner on the evening news. I shook my head in assent. All done.

He took off the apron and I got up from the chair.

Little hairs dug into my back. Pop paid him and, this is the best part, gave him a quarter for a tip. "Hey, if him ever wants to play D and D ... "

"What's D and D?" Pop asked me when we were outside.

"Losers pretending they're elves," I said, and we left.

"Any advice on women, Pop?" I asked on the way back. We walked around the lip of a pond. A duck landed, then skittered away flapped wildly. An alligator was cruising nearby.

"Marry 'em young and bend 'em to your ways," Pop replied. It seemed to me that he was the bent one, not Grandmother. "Let me give you a nickel's worth of free advice, boy. If you don't like somebody, don't look at 'em."

"What'll that do?" I asked him.

"Keep you from busting him in the chops and getting fired. Why do you think I didn't have a career in baseball? It wasn't because I couldn't play. It was because I slugged my manager, who was a lot like that twerp who just cut your hair. I glared at him in the dugout until I couldn't stand it no more. Then I hit him. End of career. I tried boxing, but I got no knockdown punch. So I ended up delivering mail. People like us always end up working for the government. You'll end up working for the government some day, too."

"No. I refuse to believe that," I said. "I hate the government."

"So do I," Pop said, laughing. "It's all owned by rich people. But it's the only place that lets a man be, and don't insist on him kissing ass all the time." He winked, and puffed on his cigar. "Just some of the time."

Back at the apartment, Sissy and Grandmother were leafing through old photos. I sat down with them on the couch. Grandmother pointed herself out in a group of young girls on a roof. "We were all underage," Grandmother told us. "They'd passed some laws about how old you had to be to work in a factory, so every time the inspectors came, we had to go up on the roof."

"How old were you?" Sissy asked. She absently reached over and scratched my back.

"Higher," I said.

"Twelve," Grandmother replied. "Look how young I was." It was sad. Her father had been first chair violinist in some Kaiser's or Tsar's orchestra. But he decided to move the family to America, where life was better. American orchestras wouldn't hire a thick-accented foreigner, however, so he ended up dead in a coal mine in Pennsylvania. Her mother had to raise four daughters and two sons alone. Then one of the sons ended up dead after eating a bad hot dog from a street vendor.

"Who's that dapper young man?" Sissy asked, pointing

to a well-dressed man in one of the photos.

"Joey Zeno," Grandmother said.

A growl emitted from across the room. Pop had dropped his *Sports Illustrated.*

"Let's not talk about him," Grandmother said, flipping the page.

"*Loverboy,*" Pop snarled. He was hot. He got up. "I'm going to the post office. You coming, boy?"

"I gotta take a shower," I said.

"Suit yourself," he said. He strode purposefully out the door, singing, "I dreamed I saw Joe Hill last night alive as you and me ... "

Grandmother said, "You two smell so festive all the time."

"Festive?" Sissy asked.

"Like Italians," Grandmother said. She pronounced it *Eye-talians.* "That grump that I married."

"What about Joey Zeno?" I asked.

"I was dating father at the time," Grandmother said, leaning back on the couch. We leaned back with her. "We had met through this awful friend of his, a union organizer named Harry. Father used to travel with him around the South, trying to organize down there. Father was muscle for him. Mostly what Harry was interested in was girls. They were back home in Cleveland and came to see the show I was in, and Harry just invites himself backstage like a big shot. Some big shot, I says to myself.

Then father comes walking in and just like that I knew what the rest of my life would be like."

We'd heard this story before. "What about Joey Zeno, Grandmother?" Sissy went. "Tell us about him."

"Oh," Grandmother said. "He was this Lithuanian fella. A new singer in our show. Very dapper, a gentleman. He took me to the opera, like I was a lady. Not like father, who took me to ballgames and smokers. I was dating both of them at the same time and father found out. You shoulda seen him. He drove around the Lithuanian parta town, looking at all the mailboxes for his name. He was gonna beat the heck outta him." She smiled ruefully. "So father came over to our house in the middle of the night, beats on the door. My mother came out with a rolling pin. We was all scared, we thought it was a prowler. My mother says, it's only that Ziska boy. I come out and father says, 'it's him or me. Choose.'" Grandmother shook her head at the memory. "I chose father. I coulda done worse."

We were mostly silent during the drive home Sunday evening. We crept through Arcadia in the dark, the AM radio fading in and out. "The choices you make," I said as we hit the final stretch of road heading into Sarasota. "Grandmother wasn't much older than I am when she married Pop."

"'I coulda done worse,'" Sissy said, slumped down in her seat. "Jesus."

Guilty of Being White

Albino peered at me in the rearview. "You decide to become a citizen all of a sudden?"

"I get a haircut twice a year, whether I need it or not," I snarled. "Oh, and fuck you." We were on our way to see *E.T., The Extra-fucking-special-Terrestrial* at the 99¢ North Trail Movierama. It was the last weekend before school started, and we were grasping for something cheap to do.

We were passing through what used to be a downtown. Back in the circus days, in the 1950's, it was vibrant. I'd seen photos. The recession had left it a dry husk filled with empty storefronts, cracked and weedy sidewalks and dying palm trees. All the action in town was at the new mall, a nightmare of commerce gone berserk.

"Notice something different?" Albino asked us. Sissy and I were in the backseat. Dave was up front with Albino, who was driving.

"No knocks in the engine?" I offered.

"You got one of those barefoot gas pedals?" Dave

said.

"You got that new car smell," I said. "The whole fucking car's clean. Except for that yellow dot on the floor ... "

"You're all idiots?" Sissy guessed. "Oh, wait ... "

Albino slammed on the brakes, and we all bounced forward. "That's right, I have brakes! The old lady took care of it. Pretty sweet."

"You carpeted the dash," I said.

"Where have you been?" Sissy asked. I shrugged and plucked the yellow dot from the floor. It was a Betty Flintstone vitamin. I crunched her down. I received a whack on the head. "Don't do that! You're not supposed to eat everything that looks interesting to you!"

Dave laughed at us. "Hey, lookie, kids," he said, and waved a flask, then showed us an elaborate flask holster strapped to his leg. His jeans were all ripped up, and there was barely enough fabric to cover his leg, much less conceal anything. He'd spelled out "Fuck You" on his black pocket tee shirt with bleach.

"The guy lives in a trailer crammed with primo weed, and this is what he brings," Sissy commented. "I'm sitting in a car bursting with potential Nobel laureates."

"Albert Junior told me where he gets his stuff," Dave said. "We could go get it wholesale, if you want."

"Where?" Albino and Sissy went.

"I'll show, then tell," Dave said. "After the movie."

The theatre was jammed with kids, oldsters, and those fucking people in between, the ones with the ulcers. Taxpayers. We had to sit in the second row with hoards of grade schoolers, who were howling like monkeys. They screamed all through the coming attractions trailers, through the ads for overpriced cinema food, and through Pepe the Jalapeño's monologue about Nachos. "*Muchismos buenos,*" Pepe assured us.

Once the movie started, Sissy and I performed an out loud running commentary:

Buzz: Elliott has a pet alien now.

Sissy: Much better than a dog.

Buzz: How so?

Sissy: Aliens clean up their own diarrhea. Especially if you zap them with a cattle prod a couple of times.

Buzz: This sounds like the voice of experience talking.

Sissy: We do live in Florida, you know. Toss a rock. You're bound to hit something alien.

Later...

Sissy: ET has the power to heal.

Buzz: ET is Jesus.

Sissy: He's Jesus and Buddha. Look at that belly.

Buzz: He's two messiahs rolled into one. Like a Reese's peanut butter cup.

Fat lady behind us, to Dave: Can you get your friends

to shut up?

Dave: No.

Albino: This is why I don't go to movies with these two.

Even later...

I got up to leave, thinking it was the end. It was satisfying because the evil government agents had murdered ET and placed his corpse in a canister, probably so they could store it with the Arc of the Covenant in that government warehouse. But it wasn't the end because ET rose from the dead.

Buzz, standing in front of the screen: You're shitting me!

Fat lady: Sit down!

Buzz, waving fist: What kind of bullshit is this?

Sissy, laughing: ET is Jesus! You were right!

Buzz: This is a cheat! It's bullshit! Just like the Bible!

Fat lady: Somebody call an usher!

Buzz, turns to audience: He is risen! Our Lord and Savior, ET! Amen!

Sissy, rolling in her seat, laughing: Praise ET!

Dave: Oh, man. I almost forgot the booze. (Pours entire flask into Pepsi cup. Drinks half.)

Buzz: ET has turned his Pepsi into cheap liquor! Another miracle!

Albino: I hate you guys.

Sissy: He's ascending into heaven! On the bars of a bicycle! Praise him!

Usher: You kids are going to have to leave.

Albino: I completely fucking hate you guys.

Buzz: I want to eat the body and drink the blood of ET.

Usher: Now you really do have to leave.

Buzz: This is the worst piece of crap movie I've ever seen in my life.

Albino: Give it a rest. And stop egging him on.

Sissy: Kiss me you fool.

Albino: Don't tempt me.

Sissy: I'm a foul temptress. Call me Sissy Magdalene. I'm gonna scrub off ET's feet with my tears and hair.

Buzz: Don't forget the Jean Naté after bath splash. Stop pushing me, I'm going.

Usher: Just get out. All of you.

We were ejected out a side door and warned never to come back. Like they could enforce something like that.

Dave said, "Look, I didn't spill a drop." He chugged down the rest of his booze.

"Where's your flask, dildo?" I asked him.

He checked his leg. Nothing but an empty holster there. "Shit! Albert Junior's gonna kill me."

"I have something important to tell you guys," Albino said.

"Speaking of Albert Junior," Sissy said, checking her purse, "weren't you gonna show us some magical place?"

"I'm serious," Albino said.

"I'm out of cigarettes," Sissy said. "We gotta stop somewhere."

"Pray to ET," I said. "He'll miracle up a pack of Winstons."

Albino kicked a can. "Fuck it," he said.

"Let's scrape together our money," Dave said. "See what we have. We're about to buy in bulk." Wallets came out. We had about twenty bucks.

"This isn't gonna cut it for buying in bulk. That's just my guess," I said.

Sissy said, "Let's go there anyway. Just for shits and grins."

"I'll drive," Dave said, holding his hand out for the keys. Albino gave them over, and slipped into the backseat. Sissy went back there with him. I sat next to Dave in the front.

"This is different," I said. "Bucket seats. I feel like royalty."

"Fuck you," Albino went.

Dave revved up the Cougar and gunned the engine. "This car is badass." He popped in a tape. *Gimme gimme shock treatment.* We squealed across the parking lot, leaving behind a trail of black. "New tires to go along with the new brakes."

"Fucking animal," Albino went. "Those tires have to last."

"Shoulda thought about that before handing me the keys, numbnuts," Dave said. We flew up the Tamiami Trail.

"So this big-time dealer lives in Bradenton?" I guessed.

"Not quite," Dave said. He took a right. We jetted across some railroad tracks, flying through the air and landing noisily.

"Cocksucker!" Albino went.

"Calm down," Sissy went.

"You don't understand," Albino said. "I have to tell you something. It's important."

"About the car?" Sissy asked.

"It's more than the car," Albino said, irritated. "It's everything."

Dave took a left.

"We're going to Newtown," I noted.

"What?" Sissy shouted. "The fuck we are!" Albino yelped.

"The fuck we is," Dave said. Newtown was the reservation for black people in Sarasota. It was built especially for them, far away from the resort areas and beaches, so that sensitive white people wouldn't have to see dark skin unless it was preceded by a knock on the door and the word, "housekeeping." Industrial parks, the airport, and a former Army Air Force base surrounded Newtown. Cops circled and prowled there to ensure domestic tranquility.

Speaking of cops, we saw the first green and white sheriff's car when we passed a 7-Eleven.

"We're gonna get busted," Albino whimpered.

"For what?" Dave said. "We're not even gonna buy anything. We're just gonna cruise past." He peeked over at me to see if I was nervous. I was a little nervous. He smiled. "See, the cops look the other way about drugs up here. Albert Junior says all the powerful dudes are getting a taste. The sheriff, the mayor, county commissioners. Just as long as it's our Negro friends who are getting narcotized and not the precious white children."

"And what do the pigs do when they see a carload of white kids driving up to Newtown?" Sissy asked.

"Shit," Dave said. "They didn't do anything to Albert Junior and me."

"Did you come in broad daylight?" Sissy asked.

"Um," Dave went.

"That's what I thought," Sissy said.

Dave took another left. "We'll drive past it real fast, then get the fuck out of Dodge."

We zipped past the entrance to Newtown. The town itself was another half-mile up the road. You could see it in the distance. "Check it out," Dave said. "It's coming up on your right."

It was one of those places where you could pull off the road onto a tiny stretch of street, and do the drop into one of three mailboxes. Standing there were four or five black guys, hands in pockets, kind of hopping around with nerves. They all had knapsacks next to them, ready to grab and run. "If you buy in bulk, like Albert Junior, you place your order about a half-hour before you drive up. When you arrive, you toss out a bundle of bills, and they toss in a bundle of weed."

Suddenly, a pair of blue and reds and sirens. "Motherfucker," Dave went.

"Now you've done it," Albino shouted. Dave pulled off onto the side of the road. A Sarasota cop car pulled in front of us. A brown sedan with a flasher on the dash pulled up behind the sheriff's car behind us. It was a cop party, and we were the guests of honor.

Albino grumbled, "Dave, you are such a dickweed. If we survive this, I'm gonna kick your ass."

"Let me do all of the talking," Dave said.

"Bullshit on that," I said.

"You don't do *any* talking," Albino said to me. "You've done enough talking for today."

A bullhorn voice said, "Turn the engine off."

Dave turned off the engine. A muzzled and harnessed German shepherd leapt out of the back of the car in front of us. The cops all emptied out. There were six of them, all big rednecks, ready to whomp on us. "Keep your mouths shut," Dave said.

The cops cautiously crept over, all spread out, like we might have a machine gun. They kept hands on hips, ready to reach for head-knocking implements, or their pistols.

"None of you are holding?" Albino asked anxiously.

"Nothing," I said.

"Nada," Sissy said.

"Nunca," Dave said.

"I just had this car fucking detailed ... " Albino started as the two doors whipped open. A big hand wrapped around my upper arm, and yanked me clear of the vehicle. I fell into a drainage ditch, slick with black mud.

"Stay down!" the cops yelled.

"This one's a girl," one cop shouted. They were all shiny metal, polyester, black leather, southern drawls and beer guts. They stood us up, and lined us side-by-side next to the road. The dog was in the car, sniffing around a bit. He leapt out a few moments later. "It's clean," his handler said, yanking the dog over to us. We had our hands laced on top of our heads.

"You need a warrant to search a car," Sissy said.

"You think you're smart, sweetheart?" a cop asked her. He got up in her face.

"Compared to what? You?" Sissy went. "Why don't

you hit me? That'll look good in court."

"This boy your brother?" the cop asked, pointing at me.

"Yeah," she said. And he punched me in the gut with the blunt end of his nightstick. I doubled over and dropped to my knees. "Your sister has a big mouth," he noted.

"Fuck you," Dave growled. "You fucking pigs."

"You say something, boy?" the cop who hit me asked. The dog sniffed at my asshole and moved on to Albino, who hadn't said a word yet.

Dave spat on the cop. And the cops rioted. They forgot about the rest of us while they knocked Dave to the ground and kicked and smacked him with their sticks. The dog bounced up and down joyfully, barking, foam dripping off his muzzle. I was curled into a fetal ball now, not hurting much. I was sizing things up. We didn't have much of a chance. My most memorable experience with cops was the night the Pizza Hut got robbed. Some kid stuck up Janet as she was walking the evening drop out to her car. He crept up behind her and stuck a pistol in her ribs. She dropped the bag, and caught sight of him running away with it, into the dark. I called the cops after Janet came inside, all shook up and stuttering. We shut down the restaurant and waited. It took them 45 minutes to show up, the fucking bastards, and it was just one prowl car with two fat rednecks inside. Janet told them what had happened, and they wrote it down on a clipboard. The younger cop accused her of doing it. She went off on the dude, putting together an impressive string of profanities. "You sound like my old drill sergeant," the older cop commented. "I am a drill sergeant," Janet snapped back. She told them how she was a disabled Vietnam veteran. Then the older cop made the younger one apologize to her. The whole time, they didn't even acknowledge my presence. I was beneath their contempt, the way I looked, the way I carried myself.

The cops pulled Dave to his feet. He was all limp, bleeding and torn. Dirt covered him. "I recognize this fucker," the big bad cop said. "He's a sex criminal." Dave had been arrested the year before for indecently exposing himself to a woman while riding his bicycle. Dave claimed he didn't mean to do it, that his swimsuit had no lining. The court didn't buy his story, so he had to do community service and go to a county shrink once a week for six months. It was the incident that started him down the trail that led to his internment at the Christian drying out clinic. He told me later on that he figured that if he was always busted for things he didn't do, he might as well do something and have fun.

"What's your shirt say, boy?" the cop asked him.

Albino interrupted. "My uncle's a lawyer."

"What?" the cop went.

"My uncle's a *Jew* lawyer," Albino said. "In Tampa. Look in my wallet."

I slowly made my way up to my feet. Sissy took my arm. The dog cop pulled Albino's wallet out of his back pocket. They pulled out his ID. "Bernstein," the cop said. "Alan Bernstein. This is you?"

"That's my uncle's name, too. Heard of him?" Albino went.

"I think I've heard of him," one of the plainclothes cops said. His knuckles were bloody. He sucked on one. "He's one of them civil rights lawyers. Good, too."

"All right," the big bad cop said. "You three git. I don't wanna see your asses up around here no more. Comprende?"

"Yes," we went, lowly. My guts were on fire. We looked guiltily at Dave.

"Don't worry, Dave," Albino said. "I'll call my uncle. We'll get you out."

Dave kind of winked at us, his eyes swelling shut, hardly a twinkle of saline left. The two plainclothes cops each took an arm and dragged him away.

We loaded in the car. Albino started up the engine and slowly pulled out onto the blacktop. Carefully, we put some miles between the cops and us.

"I didn't know you had an uncle who's a lawyer," I said, my arms still wrapped around myself.

"I don't," Albino said. He smirked at us. "Thank God for stereotypes, and the stupidity of cops. I knew those motherfuckers would fall for that. And none of 'em would admit to not knowing every Jew lawyer around."

"You better hope they don't find out," Sissy said. "Or the next time we get pulled over, it'll be a bigger shitstorm."

"That isn't gonna happen," Albino said. "Me and my mom are leaving town next week. We're going to live with her brother in Colorado Springs. He runs some kind of hippie organic food store."

"When were you planning on telling us?" Sissy asked, all pissed off. "You weren't even gonna tell me?" She grabbed his arm and shook him from behind.

"I have been trying to all day," Albino said. He reached over to her hand with his opposite hand and caressed her fingers. A light clicked on in my head. I sat back, a little stunned. "My parents are getting divorced."

"You could stay here. With your dad," Sissy said, shaky voiced.

"Naw," Albino went. "He doesn't want me. Don't worry, I'll be back in a year. I'm gonna apply to U.F., use my old address to get in-state tuition. You could apply to Florida, too, in a couple of years."

Sissy pulled her hand away from his and sat back. "I don't know. I don't know about the future."

I imagined the two of them married, having kids. Maybe living in a real city somewhere, instead of this twisted town. Albino gave me this nervous look, like I might not approve.

I smiled at him. "Look on the bright side," I said.

"With Ronnie in the White House, we could all be dead tomorrow. Then ET could heal us, and we could frolic in the radioactive ashes of this bankrupt world."

The sun dropped down into the gulf, turning the sky purple and orange. The spectacular sunset was courtesy of the phosphate mining industry, digging and grinding up underground powder and puffing it into the air, just so we could all have brighter colors and whiter whites.

"I hope Dave's all right," Sissy said.

"He's a jail veteran," Albino said. "He knows what he has to do." He pushed in a tape and hit the rewind button. "Better than any of us would anyway."

What's Your Problem?

I went over to Albino's to see him off. His dad was sitting in the living room, watching TV and drinking beer, wearing a tank top and Bermuda shorts, feet in flip flops, a smoldering stogie within reach. Bowling was on the tube. The shades were all drawn and it was dark as fuck.

"Hey, Mr. Bernstein," I said.

"Yeah," he went, not looking up. "Alan!"

Albino came out, glowing in the dark. "Where's Sissy?" he asked.

"She didn't come," I said. "Sorry, man. I tried."

"Fuck it," he said. "She deserves better than me."

"Bullshit," I went. "You want her with a lawyer, or some rich fucker?"

"Why not?" he said. "One of us should have some money. Somebody who knows how to spend it. Give me a hand."

I followed him to his bedroom. All his handbills were still up, stuck to the wall with scotch tape. All the shows we'd meant to see, but hadn't. I grabbed a box and followed him out to his car.

"Funny how your whole life can fit into the trunk of a car," he said. "Pitiful, actually." His mom's shit was piled in the backseat. A funky lamp, an old-fashioned phonograph, dresses and polyester pantsuits.

"Mom wants to get the fuck out of here right away," he said. "Oh, hey. I just remembered something." I followed him back inside, into the cramped little kitchen. He picked up a letter from the counter and handed it to me. "Here."

It was a letter to Albino from Cindy. "I don't think I should read this," I said.

"I think you should," he said.

I pulled the frayed notebook paper out and shook it flat. "How you doing, asswipe?" it began. Tasteful, tactful. Pure Cindy. "I've written Buzz three times, and he still hasn't written back. What's his deal? Why won't he write me? Please give him the attached letter."

"I don't need to read any more of this," I said. I handed him the letter back.

"I don't want it," Albino said.

"Neither do I," I said.

"Man, you should read it all the way through," Albino said. "Serious as a heart attack."

"I don't need this," I said. "Anything she says is bullshit anyway. I need to make a clean break."

"Suit yourself," Albino said. He dropped it in the trash.

I stood there for a moment, staring at it. No. I wouldn't pick it up. I'd be strong. I'd run my own fucking life.

The car horn went off. "The old lady's getting impatient," he noted. We walked outside and he got in the driver's seat. Slammed the door shut. He stuck out his hand. I shook it. "Dude," he said. "It's been real." He revved up the engine, and took off. Just like that.

I got in my van and drove over to Dave's. He was still in pretty bad shape from his beating. Albert Junior nodded at me as I walked into the trailer without knocking. "It's Buzz," I said. "The guy who knows Dave." Every time I came over, I had to reintroduce myself. He didn't even remember me from when I had helped Cindy move out. I told him about that once and all he had to say about it was, "Crazy. That bitch still have my bong? Aw, fuck it."

Dave was sitting cross-legged on a bare mattress on the floor, eating a bowl of Cap'n Crunch, and watching cartoons on a tiny black and white set. He wore a pair of ratty gym shorts and yellowed socks without any elastic left.

I sat down on the floor next to him. We watched cartoons together for a while. "How the fuck you doing?" I finally asked him.

"How the fuck do I look like I'm doing?" he went,

spitting cereal on himself and the mattress.

"Albino's gone," I said.

"Yeah," he went. "People come. People go. That's goddamned life."

I sat there for a couple minutes more, then got up. "Take it light," I said.

"The only way I take it is up the ass," Dave said, staring angrily at the set, crunching away.

My main desire in life became to antagonize as many people in life as I could. I was a sour young man, filled to the nostrils with hate, hate, hate.

At school, there was a girl named Terry, but she didn't want to be called Terry, she wanted to be called Terr-Bear. Terr-Bear always wore a tiny teddy bear above her right breast, and she was oh-so-cute. Her ambition was to have humanity love her.

Unfortunately, our ambitions clashed.

Even though I resided at a lower social stratum than she—I was at the bottom, and she was at the top—we couldn't avoid each other, ending up in some of the same classes. I treated her like I treated just about everyone, with contempt. This hurt Terr-Bear, and her big brown eyes would well up with tears at the thought that someone in this big squishy-wishy world did not find her at all likeable.

One day in social studies she sent me a note, with

a tiny teddy bear sticker at the top. A bubble from the teddy bear's mouth said, "Let's be friends!" The note asked, "Why don't you like me?"

I wadded it up and tossed it on the ground. Sister John the Baptist made me throw it in the trash.

After class, Terr-Bear had a couple of her girlfriends accost me at my locker. "How dare you not like Terr-Bear. You're a bug compared to her," they said.

"True, true. But even a bug should be free to like whomever he pleases," I said. "I choose to be Terr-Bear-Free."

"Creep," they chimed.

As they walked away, I checked out their asses, which were plump and nice.

That night, as I got off work, two football players I knew from school sauntered up to me across the parking lot.

"Nice night," one said. He was short, and his father was in the mafia and owned a seafood restaurant.

"Yeah, real nice," said the other one, who looked like a robust, young Kennedy. He and I knew each other from Pee Wee Football, which my father had forced me to play for a year, when I was eleven. The two of us were actually good friends at the time, but lost contact after I stopped playing. When I showed up at the Catholic school a few years later and saw him, I knew that I could not talk to him, or even acknowledge that we'd once been friends.

This was the first time that we would speak during high school, and the last. Later, he would go to Georgia Tech on a football scholarship and break his leg during the annual game against rival Georgia, which ended his athletic career before it even began. But, he met and married the daughter of a famous golfer and now runs his father-in-law's chain of car dealerships in south Florida.

"What did I do?" I asked, right before the two of them grabbed me by the arms and dragged me into the dark, where they beat the living hell out of me. I neither wept nor begged for mercy. I'd been taking beatings since before I could remember, and it was not even the best beating anyone had ever laid on me. After one memorable one administered by my father, I remember him saying, "Well, it's only a baby tooth. It's not like its permanent."

The son of Mafioso spat on me afterward as I lay groaning on the dewy crabgrass near the restaurant. I smelled printer's ink, and could hear the press rumbling next door.

The future car dealer said, "You hurt Terr-Bear's feelings, dude."

Son of Mafioso said, "Man, but you sure can take a beating. Nothing personal, but Terr-Bear's a friend of ours, you know."

"Uh, huh," I said.

Son of Mafioso then gave me a hand up. He dusted the wet grass off my back and helped me to my little brown

Chevy van. "You all right to drive?" he asked.

"I'm okay," I said.

"Be nice to Terr-Bear," the future car dealer warned me.

I rested my head on the steering wheel, trying to catch my breath, as I listened to their Trans Am rev up and squeal away.

The next morning in school, Terr-Bear walked up to me as I dug through my locker. She touched me on the arm. "Are you okay? I'm so sorry about what those guys did to you."

I turned to her and said, "I want to assure you that I'm madly, deeply in love with you. So please, don't send any more football players to beat me ever again. Okay?"

"Um," she said.

"I love you more than life itself, all right?"

She sniffled a bit, looked down at her Catholic school shoes.

"For God's sake, don't weep." I walked away from her, and avoided her, skipping classes for the rest of the day.

The next day, my sister caught me in the hall. She'd starting running with the popular crowd since Albino had taken off. She was working on becoming the most popular girl in school. It was not all that important to her. It was just something to do, and a way to fuck with people. She said, "I've taken care of it."

"Taken care of what?" I asked.

"No one's going to rough you up any more."

"There you go again," I said. "Looking out for little brother."

"I do what I can," she said.

We smiled at each other.

"You lack certain social graces, little brother."

"I take pride in that, sister," I said.

She licked her thumb and rubbed it on a bruise on my cheek. Her fingers rested on my ear. "Well, at least no one can see your acne with all these bruises."

"Always look on the bright side of life," I said.

"It's our motto," she said.

Over time, Terr-Bear's star dropped. She had gone too far in showing her sadistic side.

Chuck got promoted back to manager at work, and a new guy came in, an ex-Navy chief who talked a good game about running a tight ship, but didn't really care what went on as long as he didn't know about it. So I was drunk most of the time when I worked.

Sissy cut down on her hours so she could do more and more social stuff. Boys gave her money and dope and booze all the time, so she didn't really need the job anymore. We drifted apart a bit.

Christmas came. I didn't buy gifts for anyone, save a secret one for Sissy. My mother woke me up on Christmas morning to come out and open presents. I declined her offer and tried to go back to sleep. Buster slammed open the door and roared at me. He wondered where that happy kid had gone, the one who made everyone laugh.

"Don't you know?" I said, rolling over and smiling at him. "You beat him to death. Now you're left with me." I tossed the covers off, swung my boney legs out, plopped my boney feet on the floor. "This is it. This is all that's left," I said. I stood up and spread out my hands like I was Jesus Christ on the cross. "Where's your pride in workmanship?" I asked him. "How about a shot to the solar plexus to start the day?"

I turned 18, the age of majority. One more semester, and I'd be rid of the whole lot of them. Masturbatory thoughts of the day I'd walk out the door spun in my head.

I applied to the University of Florida, and was accepted. I would put two hundred miles between them and me. Two-fucking-hundred miles.

Until then, I closed the door of my room every afternoon and blasted my music as loud as I could. Then I went to work.